"PRETTY FAIR SHOOTING..."

Kilrain spun on his heel. "How the hell did you get back here?"

"On my two feet," Slocum said pleasantly.

"Well, your two feet can either get the hell out or in—in that there log house."

"I ran into a couple of riders today out by Lincoln Ford."

"What's that to do with me?" Lupis Kilrain stood hard as a fence post, staring at Slocum who wasn't giving an inch.

Nor was John Slocum giving anything. "It's got this to do with you: They could have been your men, the ones you sent to the Chicago House with that cute little doll with the big nipples." And as he said those words, his hand was close to his belt. Why not? he was thinking; why the hell not? Why not flush the son of a bitch....

OTHER BOOKS BY JAKE LOGAN

RIDE, SLOCUM, RIDE
HANGING JUSTICE
SLOCUM AND THE WIDOW KATE
ACROSS THE RIO GRANDE
THE COMANCHE'S WOMAN
SLOCUM'S GOLD
BLOODY TRAIL TO TEXAS
NORTH TO DAKOTA
SLOCUM'S WOMAN
WHITE HELL
RIDE FOR REVENGE
OUTLAW BLOOD
MONTANA SHOWDOWN
SEE TEXAS AND DIE
IRON MUSTANG
SHOTGUNS FROM HELL
SLOCUM'S BLOOD
SLOCUM'S FIRE
SLOCUM'S REVENGE
SLOCUM'S HELL
SLOCUM'S GRAVE
DEAD MAN'S HAND
FIGHTING VENGEANCE
SLOCUM'S SLAUGHTER
ROUGHRIDER
SLOCUM'S RAGE
HELLFIRE
SLOCUM'S CODE
SLOCUM'S FLAG
SLOCUM'S RAID
SLOCUM'S RUN
BLAZING GUNS
SLOCUM'S GAMBLE
SLOCUM'S DEBT
SLOCUM AND THE MAD MAJOR
THE NECKTIE PARTY
THE CANYON BUNCH
SWAMP FOXES
LAW COMES TO COLD RAIN
SLOCUM'S DRIVE
JACKSON HOLE TROUBLE
SILVER CITY SHOOTOUT
SLOCUM AND THE LAW
APACHE SUNRISE
SLOCUM'S JUSTICE
NEBRASKA BURNOUT
SLOCUM AND THE CATTLE QUEEN

SLOCUM'S WOMEN
SLOCUM'S COMMAND
SLOCUM GETS EVEN
SLOCUM AND THE LOST DUTCHMAN
  MINE
HIGH COUNTRY HOLDUP
GUNS OF SOUTH PASS
SLOCUM AND THE HATCHET MEN
BANDIT GOLD
SOUTH OF THE BORDER
DALLAS MADAM
TEXAS SHOWDOWN
SLOCUM IN DEADWOOD
SLOCUM'S WINNING HAND
SLOCUM AND THE GUN RUNNERS
SLOCUM'S PRIDE
SLOCUM'S CRIME
THE NEVADA SWINDLE
SLOCUM'S GOOD DEED
SLOCUM'S STAMPEDE
GUNPLAY AT HOBBS' HOLE
THE JOURNEY OF DEATH
SLOCUM AND THE AVENGING GUN
SLOCUM RIDES ALONE
THE SUNSHINE BASIN WAR
VIGILANTE JUSTICE
JAILBREAK MOON
SIX-GUN BRIDE
MESCALERO DAWN
DENVER GOLD
SLOCUM AND THE BOZEMAN TRAIL
SLOCUM AND THE HORSE THIEVES
SLOCUM AND THE NOOSE OF HELL
CHEYENNE BLOODBATH
SLOCUM AND THE SILVER RANCH FIGHT
THE BLACKMAIL EXPRESS
SLOCUM AND THE LONG WAGON TRAIN
SLOCUM AND THE DEADLY FEUD
RAWHIDE JUSTICE
SLOCUM AND THE INDIAN GHOST
SEVEN GRAVES TO LAREDO
SLOCUM AND THE ARIZONA COWBOYS
SIXGUN CEMETERY
SLOCUM'S DEADLY GAME
HELL'S FURY
HIGH, WIDE AND DEADLY

JAKE LOGAN

SLOCUM AND THE WILD STALLION CHASE

BERKLEY BOOKS, NEW YORK

SLOCUM AND THE WILD STALLION CHASE

A Berkley Book/published by arrangement with
the author

PRINTING HISTORY
Berkley edition/July 1987

ISBN: 0-425-09783-8

A BERKLEY BOOK ® TM 757,375
Berkley Books are published by The Berkley Publishing Group
200 Madison Avenue, New York, N.Y. 10016.
The name "BERKLEY" and the "B" logo
are trademarks belonging to Berkley Publishing Corporation.

PRINTED IN THE UNITED STATES OF AMERICA.

10 9 8 7 6 5 4 3 2 1

1

Without a sign of the sun, the morning had slipped into the sky; a gray infinity lying like a lid over the high mountain country. The spring thaw had come suddenly to the Bitterroots, and John Slocum knew he had to be the first traveler through Lolo Pass. All winter long the mountains were impassable, and Slocum saw no sign that anyone had preceded him on the slippery trail.

Now, riding his spotted pony carefully, he sniffed the wetness in the thin air, gauging each step of his saddle horse, as well as of the dun gelding he was leading by a halter rope. A good horse, the dun, serving double duty as a saddle mount when needed, and now loaded with the bedroll, the warbag, the Sharps.

Reining the spotted pony, he let his eyes go deep into the gray sky at the place where he reckoned the sun to be. It was lightening up. Now, as a thin wet flake of snow landed on the back of his gloved hand, he smiled wryly. It was still a long way to Red Butte and Boge Grady, but he didn't mind. Boge Grady could wait. Slocum had taken this shorter, more dangerous trail, not in order to save time, but because he wanted to take time, time to reflect, time to see the high rolling country of the Sapphire Range. Boge Grady and his wild horse hunt could wait.

With the snow falling faster Slocum sat his horse, very still in the mountain silence. They were well above the timberline, yet he was still checking his back trail. No one following him that he knew about, yet a man could never be too careful. Something in Bogardus Grady's note had indicated that the job he was offering could be trouble. Slocum was never offered any other kind; and he'd been wary all the way from Deer Lodge.

He lifted the reins and kneed the spotted horse, who took a step forward, pulling on the dun's halter rope, as the thin snow came slicing out of the pewter-colored sky.

Shortly, the trail bent downward and he let his mount have its head, picking down the softening trail through heavy timber. Sometimes the horses' shoes rang on bare rock. Now, with the suddenness of unpredictable mountain weather, it stopped snowing and the sky quickly cleared into a cool, dazzling blue. Slocum drew down his Stetson hat, tightened the bandanna around his neck. He allowed a shiver to run through him, interested to note that he felt it as a warning in a strange way. But he was not a man to dwell and ruminate; he let the thought have its moment, and he was again attending fully to what was before him.

Presently the trail lifted to his left and he crossed over a low neck of rock. The rock was clear of snow, and he studied the speckled moss that clung to it. He had that funny feeling now that had guided him since he was a boy, the sense of something not right. But he could see nothing, hear nothing out of the ordinary. Still, his attention quickened. He was warmer suddenly, but still kept buttoned as they crossed a large open space, the ground hard under a thin layer of softening soil. Coming around the shoulder of a huge rock, he saw two clouds on the horizon scudding away to the right.

Around the middle of the morning the sun struck over the land with a brilliant light. The spotted pony nickered low as they reached the center of the open area, and Slocum let him have his head. The animal headed immediately for a patch of green growing out of the spongy ground. Both horses were hungry and they snapped their big teeth at the grass all around them as though they couldn't eat fast enough. Watching them and studying his surroundings, Slocum found himself breathing heavily in the thin air. His nose stung from it, and his eyes were tearing at the corners. His lungs sucked deeply of the astringent air.

Suddenly the dun horse snorted, right in the middle of a bite of grass, and tossed his head high, his mane tumbling, while his ears flicked about. The spotted horse jerked his head up, taking a step backward as he did so, and stood stock still with both tawny ears shot forward and up.

Quickly Slocum loosened the thong on his holstered sixgun, ready for a fast crossdraw. His green eyes narrowed while he minutely examined the open ground, the surrounding timber, the soaring cliffs to his rear. But again he saw nothing out of the usual.

The only things moving were some small black dots

on the far bench across the valley. He reckoned them to be mustangs, wild horses, and wondered if they might be part of the herd Grady had written him about, saying he had a big contract with the army for remounts, mentioning that there'd been trouble, but leaving most of it to John Slocum's figuring. It wasn't the sort of job Slocum generally favored, but he could use the money, and felt the need for action. A man could get rusty.

The spotted pony and the dun had bent again to their feed, and the moment of alarm had passed. Lifting the reins, Slocum started them into a slow pace, still watching, listening for anything that was not a normal part of his surroundings. He was very much aware of that past moment—the snort of the dun and the twitching ears of both animals—and his own inner quickening which had so often warned him.

They rode through the fringe of spruce and pine and entered a meadow, still fairly covered with the retreating snow. It was over on the far side of the area that his eye caught something glittering as it reflected the light of the sun. He didn't ride toward it immediately, but sat still on his horse, still listening, while the animal pawed at the snow.

He looked away from the shiny object lying in the bright snow, let his eyes go deep into the blue sky as he cleared them, and cleared himself too so that he could see differently. He looked again at the meadow, seeing now that he was looking at the remains of a campsite, still largely covered with snow, yet clear too in its definition there alongside the trail.

Kneeing the horse, he rode right up to the object that had caught his attention. It was a pair of smashed field glasses, the sun having caught the lens. Dismounting, he groundhitched the horses and began to examine the area.

Near the field glasses he discovered the broken stock of a rifle. Kicking away the snow, he found wagon tracks, but no sign of any wagons. Yet the wagons had camped here, likely in the late fall, the people hoping to get through to the western slopes of the mountains before the snows closed Lolo Pass.

Kicking his way through the crust of snow that covered the wagon tracks, he worked his way to the edge of the meadow, where at a fringe of spruce and pine the land dropped into a steep canyon. Holding onto some thick brush, he leaned over as far as he could to get a clear view. Rocks, snow, and not much else lay below him. But it was clear that the wagons had gone over the edge. But why? There were two possible explanations: that the drivers had been drunk, or that somebody had ordered them over at gunpoint. He could see no actual sign of the wagons from his perch, but the tracks leading to the edge of the precipice were undeniable.

He pulled himself back up to his feet and took out a quirly and lighted it. There must have been quite a few wagons. The campsite had been a large one. Indians? It was always the first thought. Whatever, whoever it was, the action had taken place before the big snows. And maybe that had been deliberate on somebody's part, to make sure the evidence was covered at least until the spring thaw.

Behind him the spotted pony snorted. Turning, Slocum saw him backing away from something, his eyes rolling. Nearby, the dun had lifted his head and let loose a low nicker, his ears up, questioning.

Slocum's long stride took him quickly to the horses,

his hand on the butt of his Colt. There was something on the ground in front of the animals, but he couldn't yet see what it was.

He stood beside the spotted horse, who was still spooky, snorting and throwing his head and backing off. Then he saw it. It was lying in a patch of snow where the pawing horse had cleared a place to feed. It was a hand, and there was no body attached to it.

It was pretty well into the afternoon by the time he got down to the bottom of the canyon and began digging away at the snow. It took a while to uncover the first wagon, and part of another. The first body was of a man who had been shot through the head, the second had evidently been killed with an axe. He found dead horses, the remains of three or four other bodies. There were scattered bones, some coat buttons, firearms that were still fully loaded. The coyotes hadn't left much.

By the time he made his way back up to the meadow, the sun was close to the horizon. Already the air was colder, with the hard remaining snow clinging to the mountain.

That evening he camped at the other side of the meadow, away from the campsite. He had hobbled the horses, and ate his supper of beef jerky and canned peaches, and now sat in front of his small campfire in the advancing dark, drinking coffee, smoking, trying to put it together.

Yes, a big wagon train, coming from Virginia City, hoping to make it over the mountains into Idaho before the big snows. The Bitterroots ran north and south dividing Montana and Idaho, the huge mountains impassable in winter, and often in early spring. They were wild, uninhabitable; only an occasional Indian or trap-

per ventured through during the winter months. But it
was the short route west, and clearly it had been a
temptation for whoever was leading the wagon train.
But it wasn't the weather that had been the wagon
train's nemesis, nor Indians. The sign was clear. It had
been murder.

In the dying light Slocum looked about him. It was
the eastern slope of the divide and it was especially
beautiful up here beyond the Clearwater River. The
fated wagon train party must have realized the beauty
too, he thought. High mountains ringed the meadow. At
the time they must have come, in the late fall, the grass
would have still been long and rich and the stock would
have had ample feed. There was a clear, full stream
running down from the pine timber creeks above. A
more tranquil setting would have been difficult to find.
And he felt the horror lying there, half buried beneath
the snow, which by early summer would be fully re-
vealed—yet only to someone who could see it. The
deed had been well planned. Chances were it would
remain undiscovered except by the lone Indian or trap-
per to whom it would likely mean little. For himself, it
had been the most casual chance to stumble on the
grisly tableau.

That night he didn't sleep fully, but rested in that
half-asleep, half-awake state that he experienced on the
trail when he felt the need to keep especially alert. Now
and again he awakened to hear the choppy bark of a
coyote or some other sound, checking each time as to its
origin. He was up before dawn, rolling his bedding,
boiling coffee, and chewing on some more of the jerky.

He had already cinched the pack saddle on the dun
horse and was about to mount the Appaloosa when on
an impulse he swung back down to the ground. Some-

thing had caught his attention just for the moment the day before when he had found the hand, but he had not stayed with it, undoubtedly the severed hand had taken his full notice. But there had been something.

In a moment he had reached the remains of the hand. He stood looking down at those humble bones that had once been so vital a part of someone. Who had done such a terrible thing? And why? Robbery? Revenge? Maybe he would never know, but he had seen something the day before which hadn't quite registered. And for a moment he wondered if maybe he had imagined it. Or perhaps he or the horses had kicked snow over it inadvertently. But then he saw it—the little piece of metal. He bent down and picked it up.

It was a locket, and its chain was missing. He wondered at its being left there. Had it belonged to the owner of the hand? Perhaps in such a desperate encounter as dismembering another person, the killer had been in a great hurry, or possibly the locket had been brought from some other part of the campsite long afterwards, by a coyote.

He tried the clasp, but it wouldn't open. He didn't try to force it. Suddenly he felt the strong urge to get moving. It was surely no time to linger. He had seen all that was necessary. What to do about it could be decided later. He shoved the little locket into his shirt pocket and stepped up onto the spotted pony.

In the next moment he was riding out of the meadow.

2

It was about the middle of the forenoon when Slocum and the two horses rounded the big cutbank and followed the wide trail which ran alongside the creek leading to the town.

High overhead a band of geese swung through the clear sky. Watching them, he thought of the wagons westering, looking for new land, new opportunity, new life. The land was changing fast since the War, since the time of the free Indian and the mountain man. Pretty soon, he knew, even this much wildness now would be gone.

As the two horses waded the ford just outside the town he shifted in his saddle, letting his right hand brush the butt of the holstered Colt. He had the definite feeling that he was expected. To be sure, he had sent word to Bogardus Grady that he would take a look-see at the wild horse job. He hadn't been more specific than that. Yet he had the feeling that he was expected, that his arrival was in fact already known, that he was being watched. Entering the town now, he kept his eyes straight ahead, taking in both sides of the street with his peripheral vision.

The town was little different from the prairie on which it had grown. From a distance it could easily have been seen as a cluster of tumbleweeds, rocks, and earth mounds. Nor, on closer inspection, was its color much different from the tawny, lion-colored hue of the drying land on which there still lay a very little snow.

He rode slowly now past the cattle pens, the sporting houses and shanties that made up the section known as the Gold Coast. He rode with care, seeing everything, yet without moving his head very much, not looking directly at anything and so not getting caught by what he saw.

And there was the sign he had been half looking for. It was newly painted, newly hung, and it said SHERIFF'S OFFICE. But he didn't stop. There was something about the wagon train that he was still not settled on. Why had no one already discovered it? Hadn't anyone missed the party that had started out over the mountains in late fall and had clearly not arrived at their destination? And so he was of two minds about reporting what he had stumbled upon at Lolo Pass, deciding now that he would check out the town before telling the law what he had seen. The bodies had been lying out there in the mountains this good while. They could wait a while longer.

At the sign that announced a barber and bath he drew rein, dismounted, and with a quick look up and down the busy street he walked into the barber's. He still had the feeling that his arrival at Red Butte was not unexpected.

From the grimy window of the Broken Dollar Saloon and Gaming Establishment two men sat watching the street.

"He ain't changed," the man with the big red face said. "That's for sure."

"You be sure," his companion said, and his voice was as hard as the expression on his pale face.

"It's him, by God. The son of a bitch."

"Slocum."

"That is what I am saying!"

"Do not even think of getting previous with me, Dancey," said the pale-faced man, speaking around his fixed smile, and with his smooth fingers flicking ever so lightly at a bit of ash on his gray broadcloth coat.

The man named Dancey grew even more red in his flat face. He was a knobby man with tight, bowed, very powerful legs and leathery red hands. His eyes were small, while the skin on his face was stretched tight. His companion, on the other hand, was looser, smooth, coiled lightly for swift and—it was known throughout the Territory—remorseless action. It was his eyes that belied his easy manner. They were laughing eyes. Some people had seen those laughing eyes turn to nails; others wondered what Sheriff Lupis Kilrain's eyes were indeed laughing at.

The sheriff let his hand drop down to his sixgun now as a smile came to his pale face. The cold smile in that cold face seemed to emphasize the strangeness of those laughing eyes. Clyde Dancey, who had killed more than just a few men in cold blood, never felt comfortable when those "laughers," as he called them to himself, were turned his way.

"Just working here, just doing my job as deputy," he said.

"Good way to keep it, Dancey." The sheriff leaned back farther in his chair and his eyes went back to the window. "Looks like he's gone for a bath," he observed, and then added, "Or more than likely too, some news of the way of it here in Red Butte. He is no fool, from what I hear."

"That's for sure," Dancey agreed.

"You know him, do you?"

Both men were speaking without looking at each other, their eyes on the street where Slocum had entered the barber's.

"Not personal. Know *about* him. I have heerd things. He is a mean son of a bitch to mess with, is what I hear tell."

"But he had to come over the mountains. He had to come through Lolo Pass." Lupis Kilrain's voice was insistent, pinning his point.

"You figger he could've come on something?"

"I am figuring like he did come on something," Kilrain said, his tone soft with finality. He never moved his eyes from the window.

Dancey felt an unwelcome feeling pass through his body. To handle it, he said now, "But Dutch and them said they'd covered everything real good."

"They had better hope so," replied the sheriff, now turning his laughing eyes right onto his companion. "Snow melts. Am I right? And coyotes and the wolves move things about. Would you say?"

For a moment Clyde Dancey didn't know where to look. For a long moment. Then he said, "I can take care of Mr. Slocum any time you say the word."

Something flicked into the corners of Lupis Kilrain's mouth. Maybe a smile. That was the kind of talk he liked. That was how a man spelled out his place so he knew where he was, knew who was head man, knew the situation, could read the sign.

"Point is," he said, "Boge Grady don't have to benefit by the man." He watched his deputy playfully.

Dancey felt his face getting hot. "Let me handle this," he said, his face revealing his earnest discomfort, to Kilrain's great amusement. "Let me handle it." And he touched the big holstered gun at his hip with his thick forefinger.

Kilrain was shaking his head even before Dancey had finished speaking. "Not that way. It has to be . . . not obvious. I will tell you when it's time."

He lay on his back on the bed in the little room at the Chicago House, staring up at the long, twisting crack in the ceiling, at the peeling wallpaper where it met the edges of the one window, at the ancient brown water stains that mottled almost the entire room. It was hot, the air trapped in the small enclosure. He had the window wide open, and still there was hardly any movement of air. Soon it would be cool, but now it was hot. And therefore he lay absolutely still with nothing moving other than his heartbeat and his thoughts.

It was good lying there. It was what he needed. It had been a long ride over the mountains and now he needed to rest, to collect his thoughts. Even his thoughts felt tired. He lay there, allowing his tiredness to circulate through his whole body.

His thoughts centered again on the strange, grotesque little tableau of the hand reaching up through the melting snow. The hand to which nothing was attached. There was something in that . . . yes, *gesture* . . . that reaching or pointing after death that gave such a signature to the tragedy. The ghoulish gesture that seemed to be a pointing, an accusing, leaving no question but that there had been a special horror perpetrated and that what would be unfolded when the snow finally melted away would be even more than could be imagined as horror and tragedy.

Who could have done such a thing? Why? Revenge? Had there been children? Robbery? Certainly not Indians. And simple robbery couldn't account for the viciousness of the scene that had claimed him there at Lolo Pass.

And had no one come to investigate? Well, depending on the wagon train's destination, there would be search parties sent out when the train was missed at wherever its destination happened to be. In the winter nothing was possible. But now, with spring, they would definitely be missed and there would be a search. It was not unlikely that he was the only person who was aware of the event, other than the killers.

A suspicion of a breeze touched the window sill and the grimy little slip of a curtain moved gently, then returned to its absolute stillness. Of course, he should report it to the law, yet he hadn't. Why hadn't he ridden right to the sheriff's office and told what he had stumbled upon out at Lolo Pass? Something had stayed the action, some inner voice had cautioned. He had not really even thought about it, but had simply refrained from any move in that direction.

Well, he could wait, he could think it over, but not for too long. The longer he waited, the longer he remained silent about his discovery, the more vulnerable he became if it ever came out that he had been at the scene of the crime. For why wasn't he reporting it to the law?

Suddenly he remembered the little locket he had picked up and put into his pocket, and how he had wondered if it had belonged to the owner of the hand. He reached now to his shirt pocket and brought out the small gold locket. It was cold from its long journey. He tried again to open it, but it was stuck. He was about to look for something to force it, the blade of his throwing knife, when he heard a step in the corridor outside. He sat up instantly, swinging his feet to the floor, reaching for his sixgun.

The knock was soft, almost hesitant, and a muffled voice said his name.

Slocum was barefoot but still in his shirt and trousers. "Who are you?" he demanded.

"Mr. Slocum, I've got a message for you." It was a woman speaking.

"Tell it through the door, or shove it underneath," he said.

"Please let me in. I am alone. I need your help."

He hesitated. Swiftly stepping to the window behind him, he checked that there was no one setting up a backshooting. Then he stepped back to the door and with his left hand unlocked it.

"Come in," he said. "Slowly."

The girl who walked in couldn't have been more than twenty-four. She was tall, dark, with a figure under white satin that brought Slocum's instant attention. When her eyes dropped to his trousers he felt his loins beginning to pound.

"What can I do for you, honey?" His words were not as hard as they had been, but he had not relaxed his vigilance. It was an old ruse that he could easily be walking into.

"I've come to welcome you to Red Butte. Compliments of Sheriff Lupis Kilrain."

"Shut the door."

Without turning away from him she pushed it shut. There was a smile in the corner of her mouth as she stood in front of him, quite at ease, her eyes moving over his body, resting on the bulge in his trousers.

"You can see why I couldn't really get myself under the door or send my message with just words."

Slocum grinned at her. "You can tell the sheriff I appreciate the hospitality." Stepping quickly behind her, he locked the door.

"I'll tell him," she said. Her smile was dancing all over her face now. "But what am I going to tell him when he asks me how it was?"

"I see what you mean."

"Do you?"

"I wouldn't want you to tell him anything but the truth."

"The whole truth."

"And nothing but the truth."

He had reached over, still holding his sixgun, and was unbuttoning her dress at her waist.

Suddenly she reached down and pulled the dress up over her head. She stood before him totally naked, her cheeks flushed, the nipples of her beautifully formed breasts long and hard as they pointed darkly upward.

Slocum found his breath coming hard as he took it all in.

"May I?" She took a step forward when he didn't answer and, reaching down, unbuckled his belt. His trousers dropped to the floor and he stepped out of them. With her hand gripping his erection she led him to the bed. Sitting down on the edge she took him deep into her mouth and throat.

Slocum thought he would go mad. She had brought him almost to his limit when he pulled out and spread her on the bed, driving all the way up into her while she squealed with delight. Together they thrashed the bed, almost bringing it to collapse as they danced their bodies faster and faster until at last reaching the impossible, exquisite moment when together they came.

They lay entwined in utter exhaustion for a long, long moment. And finally, when they slowly disentangled she said, "My God, are you still holding that damn gun, for Christ sake."

Slocum raised up on an elbow and grinned down at her, his eyes sweeping over her fantastic, sweating body.

"Honey, I do love to screw. But I love to go on living even better."

She had a moment taking that in, then she laughed. "There isn't anybody out there."

"That's what I know."

"Then if you knew, why the gun?" She had stretched her long arms over her head and was pointing her toes toward the foot of the bed.

Slocum's grin broadened, hardened a little as his green eyes studied her. "Maybe it's not easy to get it, honey. But, see, the reason there's nobody outside is just *because* I kept hold of my gun." He gave a short laugh. "But don't break your head over it."

She shook her heard, sighing. "Crazy."

"That's right," he said. "It's crazy."

Her hand had dropped down along his stomach and was just brushing his stirring organ.

"I want more," she said, and slid her thigh over on top of him.

In the next second he had rolled away from her and was out of the bed and up on his feet. "You say one word and I'll blow your head off," he said quietly.

"What are you talking about? I never..."

Slocum quickly pulled on his pants. Reaching under the bed, he drew out the nasty-looking cutdown Greener 12-gauge. Sidling quickly to the window, he looked out, from an angle so that no one outside could see him.

Then he heard it again. It was almost a breathing, and it came from out in the corridor.

"You can let the boys in if you want," he said with a cold grin. His eyes had turned to green ice and he watched her terror.

"I—I don't know what you mean."

"The sheriff's boys. They're outside. They want to play. Or is it the sheriff's boys? Maybe it's somebody else?" He studied her as she began hurriedly to dress.

"I don't know what you're talking about," she said.

"Next time," he said, as she started toward the door, "next time, don't bring your friends. I'll guarantee you a real good time. But I'll expect the same."

"You'll get it. I guarantee it, Slocum," she said. "But I didn't—"

"Shut up. Just tell those boys out there, if they even get close enough for me to smell them I'll by God cut 'em right off at the pockets." And he pointed with the Greener.

Her hand was shaking as she touched the doorknob.

"Come again," he said.

"I'd really like to, Mr. Slocum," she said with a smile that had meaning in it.

"You have a name?"

"Call me Sweetheart. Sweetheart Moon."

"Make it jacks or better," the dealer announced, smothering a belch as his slim white hands broke out a new deck. He removed the joker, mixed the cards, shuffled, and cut in total silence under the casual eyes of the men seated around the green baize-top table.

The dealer's middle finger on his left hand was missing, and so was his left eye; at any rate, he wore a black patch over it. His name was Harold the Professor, and it became immediately evident to Slocum as he sat at the table that neither the lack of the finger nor eye proved in the least detrimental to the Professor's ability to skin his playmates. Harold's hands were as smooth as silk, his good eye as sharp as a snake's, and as stony. The expression on his face was unnameable. As the tides of fortune moved back and forth across the table he remained impassive as Justice.

Slocum knew that the best places to obtain information without exciting comment were the saloon, the barbershop, and the sporting house. These were the rialtos where, under relaxation and need, pleasure evoked gossip that could change a man's life, or his death.

For a while the game proceeded in desultory fashion. Slocum won a couple, lost a couple. His purpose wasn't to build his bankroll, but to get the flavor of the town, plus anything he could pick up on Bogardus Grady and his wild horse hunt. Not to mention the lost wagon train. He was surely glad he hadn't gone to the law. His encounter with Sheriff Kilrain's emissaries in his hotel room justified his action all the way. He smiled inwardly as he remembered the girl's surprise at his holding his Colt in one hand while they had at it. Of course she hadn't understood that it was that action that had kept him alert to anyone out in the corridor. And thank God for that.

Somebody ordered another round of drinks. Slocum was nursing his whiskey. He never indulged while playing cards, and only drank to keep it friendly. He lifted his glass now, his eyes searching the room.

It was a big room, plain, and wholly functional. No big chandeliers or other rich appointments the way it was in the fancy places in Denver and K.C. The bar consisted of planks supported by packing crates. There was a large mirror in back of the bar, and alongside it a massive nude reclining on a sofa with a flower arrangement covering her crotch.

The Antelope was a lively spot, filled now with smoke, the crash of laughter, swearing, the tinkle of the honky-tonk piano, the sour smell of men. There were three monte tables, a wheel of fortune purring on the wall, and as many poker games as demanded; and there were faro, dice, chuck-a-luck, and other assorted means to facilitate the exchange of money.

A fat little drummer named Willie from Kansas City joined the game.

"Take a seat," Harold the Professor greeted the newcomer sourly, while Kansas City Bill as he called himself, grinned back good-naturedly and took the chair just vacated by a government man who was contracting beef for the railroad.

Another chair was vacated in a moment, so Slocum got up from his seat next to the Professor and took it. He had been studying Harold closely, figuring the dealer was going to clean out the fat drummer, and he wanted to be in a strategic position to join in the winnings.

Several rounds passed before his chance came. He was sitting to Harold's left, and the drummer who was going to get stripped sat to the right.

"Let's make it draw poker," the Professor said, picking up a new deck and again removing the joker. He dealt swiftly, his pale white hands shiny beneath the overhead lamp.

Slocum passed. The next four players also passed, making five in all. The drummer, the sixth player, opened with a ten-dollar bet. The Professor came out with a twenty-dollar raise. Slocum called. The dealer showed not the slightest emotion at this, though Slocum knew he hadn't planned for more than one player to draw against him. The drummer called, which was according to Harold's plan.

Slocum drew one card.

"Gonna win it, are ya?" the Professor said in his vinegar tone.

Slocum didn't answer. He never talked idly while playing poker, only announcing his bet and the showdown when it was time.

Willie took three cards.

Harold the Professor said, "I play these," meaning he was standing pat.

Willie the drummer, after a quick look at his cards, checked.

Without a moment's hesitation Harold bet fifty dollars. Slocum took a card and raised him a hundred. He didn't have a thing, but he knew the dealer was bluffing. He was sure Harold was standing pat on a bust. Willie didn't matter, having checked. Even if he had helped his hand he would hesitate to call, with Slocum taking one card and raising.

The drummer showed his openers—two kings—and

folded. The Professor shook his head sadly. "Lucky bugger," he said, and threw in his hand. "Shit, drawing one card with all that money going."

Slocum tossed his hand into the discards and drew in the pot quickly. He could feel Harold's eyes on him, making a new appraisal.

One of the cowboys seated across from him stood up and stretched. It was at this moment that a big, bony man with a big, underslung jaw mostly covered with beard stubble stepped up to the table. Without a word or even a nod to anyone he sat down.

Slocum could see right away that Harold didn't like it. The man with the big jaw wasn't anyone he recognized from the crowd at the bar or at the gaming tables, and he wondered what the dealer's play would be.

"Have a seat," Harold said with a malevolent glare at the bony man.

"The name is Turk," the newcomer said. "Turk Nosniffer."

"Jesus," muttered Harold and began to deal the cards viciously.

"I be Sheriff Kilrain's new deppity." He drew back his vest to show the tin star.

"You look like Big Jaw to me," Harold said, his one eye darting venom.

There was the scrape of chairs as two of the players, including Willie the drummer, pushed away from the table.

"I have come here to play cards," Big Jaw said. "Not to daylight any of you. So let's get playing."

"Shit," Harold said. He signaled the other players to move back to the table.

Slocum was watching the dealer, who now half turned to him and winked, then rolled his one eye, indicating that the man with the star was loose upstairs.

"You be Slocum," Big Jaw said as Harold swiftly dealt and everyone relaxed.

Slocum said nothing. He felt the men at the table stiffen again. He kept his silence. The little group relaxed once more.

Harold the Professor's nine fingers flew through the deck of cards. "Stud is the game, provided nobody objects."

"Stud it is," Big Jaw agreed amiably. He was very broad in the shoulders, had thick hands studded with huge knuckles, and his prominent cheekbones created shadows in his face. He was dark; he certainly gave the impression of being crazy. As well as mighty strong.

The game opened high and fast with Big Jaw and Harold just edging out the first four pots evenly.

On the fifth hand, Slocum dealt and Big Jaw won on a full house. He also won the next round. Then Harold the Professor raked in a pot, after which a cowpoke seated next to Big Jaw won. By now the table had attracted a crowd, and Willie the fat drummer had given up his seat to a cowboy and was standing watching the play.

On the second round of the next hand Slocum, still dealing, had a king showing. He knew this was going to be the big pot, and he sensed the crowd was aware of it too. It was Big Jaw who was hanging right in. Big Jaw might have been loose in the head, but he sure knew what he was doing with those cards. Slocum could smell it. Was that why he was wearing that tin star? Or maybe it was the gun. Maybe Big Jaw was crazy enough to go all the way on a showdown. He'd known men like that. They didn't give a damn whether they lived or died; they were already in some other place in

their heads. But he had no time for such thoughts now.
So far he'd seen nothing in Big Jaw's manner that could
tip his play. The deputy was cool as a breeze under his
slight shaking, his twitches, his rapid blinking. He
hardly spoke, smoking his cigar with vigor.

Big Jaw had an ace showing and he bet three hundred
dollars. Everyone else was out now, and when it came
to Slocum he called and raised three hundred.

Big Jaw was drinking carefully. At one point Slocum
caught a spot of color darkening the deputy's face, when
he cut the deck and shoved it back across the table. At
this moment the players and spectators were totally silent. No one present was missing a move.

Still Slocum had noticed something about Big Jaw.
He was dealing with a ringer, he knew, and he had a
giveaway; he knew that too. But what was it? There was
something he had definitely seen, but somehow he
hadn't placed it. There'd been a lot going on, plus the
surprise at realizing that the big, gangling, loose-jawed
giant with the big knuckles and floppy elbows and knees
waa as sharp as a razor with those cards.

Suddenly Big Jaw spoke, his slow, hog-wallow accent dumping onto the table. "Shore hate to take 'vantage of yuh, Slocum, there, but I got me a pahr of aces,
and your kings cain't beat me 'less you ketch yerself
'nuther. How much you got there, eh?" And with a huge
elbow planted on the table, Big Jaw leaned over, cock-
ing his head slyly, all full of fun.

Catching that laughter and triumph in the deputy,
Slocum suddenly saw it. That brief spot of dark color in
Big Jaw's face, and he remembered how it was there
when he'd cut the deck and passed it back for the deal.

By hot damn, he was thinking, *by damn, that son of
a bitch; slicker'n a snake's hips*. And he knew for sure

this was the play that was going to open it for him in Red Butte. The thought of Boge Grady flashed across his mind. Was he getting sidetracked here?

But there was no time for thought now. He counted out his chips, saying, "Two thousand." Without waiting for Big Jaw to say a thing, he pushed the entire pile into the middle of the table. He could feel the rustle of excitement passing through the onlookers.

For a split second he saw Big Jaw was staggered. But it was gone, and he was himself as he matched the bet. Inside, in that great cave of a body, it seemed to Slocum he had no nerves at all, though outside he continued to twitch, scratch, spit, and clear his lumpy throat. And Slocum had seen him color twice now.

Big Jaw's long face creased even deeper into those long gulleys that ran down his cheeks. Slocum wondered if he was smiling. "Awright, awright. Deal 'em!" And he turned his hole ace over to show he was honest.

Slocum dealt swiftly, his hands clean and light over the deck, Big Jaw's eyes right on top of them. On the fifth round Slocum caught a third king. All that Big Jaw came up with was a pair of aces.

It was then he caught the spot of color again in the deputy's face. Big Jaw was looking off to the side, slightly behind Slocum. Then he moved his eyes back quickly to the game. But it was enough. Now Slocum could see the two men reflected in the mirror behind the bar. They were standing together just inside the door of the saloon. He dropped his eyes quickly so Big Jaw wouldn't know he'd spotted the setup. And he reached for the pot.

"Just a minute, Mr. Slocum." The "mister" was stuck in that sentence like a shovel.

"Just a minute," the huge man repeated, and he

leaned forward, heavy on the table with both forearms flat, his finger point at Slocum. "That third king was deep in the deck. I seen it flash when you riffled the cards, an' I cut light."

"So you did," Slocum said, and his voice was suddenly as hard as the deputy's jaw. "You took an advantage in cutting light and the king wasn't there where you thought it was." And he reached out again and pulled in his winnings, keeping his eyes fully on the other man, yet with part of his vision on the two men in the mirror. They hadn't moved from the doorway, but Slocum could tell they weren't missing a thing.

"I want to see that deck, Slocum!"

The crowd around the table had moved back considerably, but they remained on the scene, as it were, watching every move, ready to drop to the floor if necessary to avoid trouble.

"Since there be four kings in the deck, Slocum, and three landed in your hand, there is then reason to figger the fourth king cropped up." Big Jaw's voice was purring like a mountain lion. Every inch of him was furious. His eyes were blinking faster than ever, and he was clearing his throat after nearly every other word.

With absolutely no expression on his face, solemn as a judge pronouncing sentence, Slocum handed over the deck for Big Jaw's inspection. The fourth king was six cards from the bottom.

"That proves you slipped yerself that third king," Big Jaw said, his tone flat as a hammer.

Even the silence deepened now as those circling the table froze. It was a long moment.

Without any movement showing outside, Slocum shifted his weight inwardly, ready for ultimate action on the instant. Now his words fell like ice into the silence.

"It proves that you tried to bury the king so it wouldn't crop up." And he added, "Big Jaw." His green eyes were glittering as he stared right into the big man opposite him.

Slocum had dropped his hands below the table, feeling the onlookers drawing back even more now. He kept his eyes right on Big Jaw, but still aware of the two who now had moved in from the door and were spreading out to have a wider cover on him.

A full moment seeped through the gaming room as Slocum watched his words working in Big Jaw's face.

Then Slocum, catching a slight movement of Big Jaw's right hand, said, "I would not try that." Now, speaking more loudly, "Better keep those hands right where they are on top of the nice table. I have got an Arkansas throwing knife just inches from your crotch. One funny move and you'll start speaking with a squeak, my friend."

In the stiff silence that followed those words, all heard the thump of the knife blade hitting the underside of the round card table. Slocum was watching the color trying to seep back into Big Jaw's face. He was still holding the two men in the mirror in his line of vision as they slipped closer to the little tableau in the center of the room.

Harold the Professor suddenly ripped out a great sneeze. Wiping his nose with a huge red bandanna, followed by the back of his hairy hand, he said, "Reckon I will wet my tongue." And he stood up. Carefully.

Big Jaw hadn't moved. But his long cheeks had turned gray, his black eyes burned at Slocum. His hands had begun to twitch.

"I don't believe you got a cutter down there, Slocum."

"There is a way to find out." He allowed a beat and then said, "Now git, before your two friends amble over here and maybe make me nervous."

Big Jaw didn't hesitate. He stood up, looming above the table, just as Sheriff Lupis Kilrain and Clyde Dancey walked up behind Slocum, who was watching them openly in the mirror now. Both lawmen were armed, and Dancey's right hand was close to his gun butt.

"I am Sheriff Kilrain. I want you to bring your hands up onto the table."

"I don't mind, Sheriff," Slocum said pleasantly. He slowly brought his hands up and placed them on the card table. He was holding a pocketwatch. A sigh of surprise went up from the onlookers as they saw the bluff, and Big Jaw flushed all over his face.

"Well, I'll be . . ." Clyde Dancey said as he and the sheriff now faced Slocum, who was still seated.

"You're under arrest," Kilrain said.

"What for? Scaring this clown you call a deputy?"

"No." Lupis Kilrain was standing hard right in front of Slocum. His hand was on the butt of his sixgun, and so was Clyde Dancey's on his. "No. You're under arrest on suspicion of the murder of Morgan McCone and his wagon train at Lolo Pass."

"Jesus Christ." The words fell softly from John Slocum.

"He ain't gonna help you outa this'un," said Big Jaw Turk Nosniffer.

3

There was a loose floorboard just inside the doorway of the sheriff's office and the first thing that happened when the party of lawmen and their prisoner arrived was that Big Jaw Turk Nosniffer stepped right on it, lost his balance, and his boot broke through the partially rotted floor.

"You dumb shit, watch that!" snapped Kilrain.

"I didn't do it on purpose, for Christ's sake!" wailed Big Jaw.

"Shut up!" The sheriff spat swiftly in the direction of an overloaded cuspidor, missed, but paid no notice.

Thus far Slocum had been fairly amused by the turn events had taken. The accusation was so patently outrageous he almost had to laugh out loud. At the same time, he knew the situation was deadly serious. Clearly,

29

Kilrain was no man to take lightly. The question was, why him? Why Slocum?

"What proof do you have?" he demanded suddenly as the sheriff and his two deputies stood facing him in the low-ceilinged room.

"Suspicion," Kilrain snapped. "We have got suspicion. You rode in over Lolo Pass."

"How the hell else would I come in from the east? Only other trail is in from South Duro. So you spotted me riding in and you're looking for a suspect. Why?" The last word cut out of his mouth like a whip and his eyes burned into the sheriff of Red Butte.

"I will ask the questions, Slocum."

"And what's more, you know my name. How is that? What are you trying to pull, Kilrain? You and these clowns!" His eyes swept Big Jaw and Clyde Dancey contemptuously. He had taken a short step toward the sheriff, who didn't move.

"You'll get a chance to prove your innocence when the circuit judge comes. Meanwhile, I want to know why you didn't report what you saw out there at Lolo Pass."

"How do you know I saw anything?"

"Big Jaw here was following a trapline out on Ponus Ridge and he seen a rider. It's a long ways, but he had his glasses. Rider on a spotted horse leading a dun pack animal. He rode right in and reported to me."

So they had somebody out on patrol from time to time. They knew about the wagon train all along.

"So you already knew about the wagon train."

"Discovered just a while back. Didn't do any burying on account of you can't cut an inch in that ground. Waiting for the thaw. Why Big Jaw was especially interested in conditions in Lolo Pass."

"Bullshit."

"You might like to see it that way, Mr. Slocum, but meanwhile you can be cogitatin' on it in that there cell, which my deputies will take you to right now." The lean gray face suddenly found a whole new set of wrinkles, which Slocum took to be a grin. "You won't be lonesome. You got company."

For another moment Slocum stayed looking at Lupis Kilrain, sizing up the man. He was wiry, fast; he had all the marks of a killer. And he noted the new rigging at his left hip, from which the butt of a Navy Colt was easily maneuverable. But why new rigging, he wondered. The way Kilrain stood, moved, reached for the papers to build a smoke, he was obviously right-handed, not a lefty, and his gun wasn't rigged for crossdraw.

"Move it," Big Jaw said. His companion, Dancey, poked his thumb into the prisoner's shoulder.

The next thing that happened was almost quicker than the human eye could record. Dancey was flat on his back on the floor, as a result of an elbow driven almost through his guts followed instantaneously by a chopping blow behind his ear. He was out cold.

"Really coldcocked him, didn't you," Lupis Kilrain said calmly as his left hand pointed the .45 right at Slocum's belly.

"One more like that and we'll count you as a former resident of Red Butte." He motioned with the sixgun. "Through that door." Stepping over his motionless deputy without a glance at the man, he snapped at Big Jaw, "Unlock it, but watch that little son of a bitch in there. He'd slicker a nun out of her drawers on a Sunday morning."

• • •

"Welcome to Red Butte," said the little man who was lying flat on his back on one of the two bunks in the small cell. He was wearing steel-rimmed spectacles.

Slocum nodded, his eyes sweeping the room. The jail was a small log cabin at the rear of the sheriff's office with a flat roof and no window. "There are but two possibilities of escape," said the man on the bunk, "the door, which is heavily padlocked, or digging through hard ground with your fingers. Of course, if you have friends there is the chance of rescue. Otherwise, my good friend, my name is Felix O'Toole." He rose suddenly, swinging short legs to the floor, and stood before Slocum, who was head and shoulders taller. "Pleased to make your acquaintance, Mr. Slocum. Indeed, I've been patiently awaiting your arrival."

Slocum's eyebrows raised. "Expecting me?"

The little man nodded. "Big Jaw also has a big mouth, especially when plied with strong spirits. Would you care to join me?" Reaching down to his bunk, he drew forth a bottle of brown liquid. "Trade whiskey, but it's the best one can do under the circumstances. Big Jaw has promised me a better brand this evening."

Slocum, seating himself on his bunk, accepted the bottle gratefully. It was raw, but it warmed him. There was, of course, no fire in the cabin. Now, as if by signal, both prisoners seated themselves on their bunks. Slocum had a moment to study Felix O'Toole. He was a chunky little man, giving the appearance of being as broad as he was tall though this would have been an actual exaggeration. He was dressed in fine broadcloth, though Slocum noted that the material was well worn.

"What are you in for?" Slocum asked.

"A misunderstanding, sir."

"That's just what I figured. But whose misunderstanding? Yours or theirs?" He nodded his head toward the door of their small jail.

A wan smile appeared at the corners of his companion's little face. Felix had his hair cut short and he was clean-shaven. He said, "I believe the misunderstanding was mine, sir. In my failing once again to realize the abysmal depths of depravity to which my fellow human can go."

"Like?" Slocum had taken out a quirly and was lighting it.

"Like trying to horn in on somebody else's good business deal. You better know it, Mr. Slocum, this sheriff and his deputies are as crooked as the horn on a mountain sheep."

"I did figure that, young feller."

"I have got to get out of here on account of my lady friend is expecting me."

Slocum cut his eye fast then at Felix O'Toole. The little man didn't look rich enough to have a woman in this womanless country, nor was he exactly a Casanova type. What was he talking about?

"Like you know," Felix said, "women are hard to come by out here in the Territory."

"'Less you got the money," Slocum said easily.

"I don't fool myself that I am the handsomest man in the whole of the Wild West," Felix O'Toole said, "but I could be one of the richest."

Slocum sighed and smiled slightly. He had heard the old story so many times.

But O'Toole was ahead of him. "I see, sir, that you are figuring it's the same old story. Dreams of acquisition in the future. A gold mine, a hidden cache of wealth, a sudden bonanza." He waved his hand, a patronizing smile filling his moonlike face. "Sir, the fact is

I have the money at hand. Not money, let me correct myself. No, not money. Not gold. But wealth. I have great wealth, and right at my fingertips." He was grinning broadly as he began to spread his secret, rather like a small boy.

"I'd rather know how come Kilrain and his two hounds were expecting me in Red Butte. You seem to know something about that. Tell me what you know. I don't believe it was just Big Jaw happening to spot me."

Felix O'Toole shrugged two or three times, as though trying to fit himself more snugly into his broadcloth coat. Though old, the coat appeared to be new to him, at least this was the thought that passed through Slocum's mind as he watched.

"I heard them talking. They were expecting you, and it has nothing to do any wagon train. I don't know what that part is. It's got to do with somebody name of Grady."

"Figures." Slocum grinned appreciatively as he received the news. "Yep, that figures. And then by luck they saw me riding in from Lolo Pass, knew I had to come by the wagon train. And they figured they could use that to bugger up whatever they wanted with Grady. You hear anything about a wild horse gather?"

The little man shook his head. "No. Only the name Grady along with yours. Seems they don't want you and Grady, whoever that is, getting together."

"That is sound figuring," Slocum said, and his companion's grin seemed to split his little round face in half.

Slocum was studying O'Toole carefully. "You look like you swallowed the canary."

"I need a partner," the little man said.

"As you can see, I am already engaged." Slocum's eyes swept the log room.

"First we have got to get out. But I could put your talents to good use, sir. I have heard of John Slocum." He held up his hand quickly to stay any remark. "Nothing personal, let me swiftly assure you. But a man of probity, honor, and—I have been told—swift retaliation in the event of injustice to his person." A soft chuckle ran down his round cheeks and he beamed at Slocum from behind his steel-rimmed spectacles.

Slocum sat down on the edge of his bunk, then stretched out. He was now only half listening to the other man. His thoughts were going swiftly over the events of the last couple of hours. It was clear that he was marked as a friend of Boge Grady's and there was therefore, in the sheriff's eyes, a black mark against his name, and that he was being tied in with the fate of the wagon train. He had no idea what was burning the sheriff of Red Butte about Boge Grady and his wild horse hunt, but the tying in with the wagon train was something definitely to be avoided. He was being held "under suspicion," the scapegoat either for the actual destruction of the wagon train party, or simply as something with which to attack Grady. Or both. In either case, the healthy thing was to get moving. People did not take kindly to murdering people out in the mountains and leaving them for the wolves. There would be relatives and friends who would seek revenge. Hell, this was big trouble, and the sooner he got out of here the better. The only question was how.

"I am thinking it right with you," Felix O'Toole said. "How we gonna get out of here?"

"You tell me," Slocum said as he began examining the log walls of their prison.

"I got an idea," O'Toole said and he began pulling off his boots. "Money talks. You have heard the expression." To Slocum's astonishment, as he pulled off his boot a shower of gold coins fell to the floor of the cabin.

"I think I've got enough eagles here to give us a chance."

Slocum bent down and picked up one of the ten-dollar gold pieces and examined it.

"Beautiful, ain't it?" said Felix O'Toole.

Slocum nodded, tossing the coin onto the other man's bunk. "You got enough of those eagles to fly yourself out of here, have you?"

"Both of us," was the cool reply. "Providing you decide to throw in with my enterprise."

"Which is?"

"Making money."

It took a second and Slocum caught it. "You do good work," he said.

Felix smiled modestly. "Old-world craftsmanship," he said with a touch of pride. "I learned from a master."

Too late, they heard the sound at the door. Before Felix could sweep the coins out of sight Big Jaw Turk Nosniffer barged in carrying a tray of food.

"This here hotel serves the best vittles this side of the Bitterroots," Big Jaw said as he set the tray down in the middle of the floor.

"Did you bring me what I asked for?" said Felix O'Toole blandly.

"That I did." There was a strange grin on Big Jaw's face as he removed the bottle from inside his jacket and handed it to Felix O'Toole. He didn't look at Slocum.

"And what about the other?"

"What about it?" Big Jaw was looking down at the gold eagles lying on the dirt floor.

"I was just counting them," Felix said coolly. Bending down, he picked up the ten-dollar gold pieces.

Then, emptying his other boot, he handed a sizeable stack of coins to the deputy. "That's my part."

"It'll be sundown in less'n a hour. This here," Big Jaw indicated the door with his thumb, "will be un-locked. I'll fix it up after you're out. Go down to the livery. There's an old geezer name of Jules. I'll handle him. Take the blue roan what you rode in on, and he'll take his spotted horse. Leave the dun. You're gonna travel light."

"Good."

Then, with a nod, still refusing to look at Slocum, he was gone, pulling the door shut behind him and locking it.

Felix O'Toole's grin just about reached both ears. He clapped his hands together and danced a little jig. "Told you, didn't I? Heh-heh! Money talks. And, by jingo, Felix O'Toole knows what makes the mare go!"

"Calm yourself, and stay away from that door," Slocum said hard.

"What d'you mean? The man said we could go soon as it's sundown—any time now. And we'll take off like the big bird. Easy as licking a penny jawbreaker."

"That's for sure. Easy as licking a penny jawbreaker and getting your guts blown to hell."

The little man's excitement suddenly drained right out of him. He stopped in mid-stride, standing stock-still, his face very white. "What are you saying, mister? What are you getting at? You mean they are not on the up and up, the sheriff and Big Jaw and that other hooli-gan?"

"Didn't you tell me that yourself, young feller? You go out that door and you're a dead man. This setup stinks all the way to Cheyenne. Prisoners break out of jail, killed in the attempt by loyal deputies. They must think we're pretty dumb." He looked at his companion. "Well, hell take it, half of us is!" And he had to grin at the crestfallen face of his small cellmate.

"Shit!" said Felix. "What are we going to do now?"

"We're going to use our heads. And we don't have a lot of time. They'll soon figure we're on to them when we don't come out." He sniffed.

There was a chair with no back. Slocum had pulled it into the center of the room and now stood on it to explore the ceiling.

"It's sod, like I thought. Pretty well packed, but we might make it." He had taken the throwing knife which had been strapped around his leg under his trousers and was probing with it.

"How come they didn't take that off you?" Felix asked, his mouth hanging open as he strained to see what Slocum was doing.

"Lucky. They probably didn't believe I really had it when they saw how I slickered Big Jaw with my horologe."

"It's about dark now," Felix said, squinting through a tiny hole in the log chinking. "Big Jaw will be unlocking the door."

Slocum stood down from the chair. "Light the lamp," he said. "We'll make like everything is as it should be. But you stay listening by the door. We don't want them walking in suddenly."

Now he climbed back up onto the chair and began cutting into the sod roof. In moments he was sweating. It was hard work, but he was getting somewhere, hacking out clumps of dirt and straw and dried manure.

"How much time we got?" Felix asked, his voice anxious now as the truth of their situation began to reach him.

"We've got the time we've got," Slocum said. "Not much." The sweat was running down his face, and was even bothering his grip on the knife. But finally he had cut a hole through which he could pull himself up onto the flat roof.

"It's ready," he said, lowering his aching arms and looking down at Felix O'Toole. "You want to go first?"

"No, I don't. Can't they see us against the sky?"

"If they're looking, more than likely they'll see us."

"Jesus . . ."

"I'll go first, then. You take that lamp and begin spreading coal oil over the door. Then light it when I tell you. Then you get your ass up here quick as you can. I'll try to pull you up."

"Gotcha."

"Don't head for the livery. They'll maybe have their horses out in front of the office at the hitch rail. We'll take them."

"Gotcha." The word came as a gasp as O'Toole began spraying the coal oil over the wooden door.

"Hurry."

"Done."

"Now throw the lamp and get up here. Fast. I'm going through."

He had pulled himself halfway through the hole in the roof and was supporting himself with his forearms and elbows when he heard the glass break as Felix threw the lamp and the sheet of flame lit up the front of the log jail. Then he was up and through, and lying flat on the roof, reaching down grabbing Felix's wet, eager hands, and pulling him up.

It was then they heard the shots, the drumming of horses' hooves, men yelling. They were both running along the roof, dropping down on the side away from the street, and then running around to the front of the sheriff's office, with Slocum in the lead.

There were three horses at the hitch rack. They mounted quickly, and Slocum reached down and freed the third animal, slamming him over the rump to spook him away. Then they were galloping down the main street with a posse of horsemen following. It seemed to have sprung from nowhere.

"What the hell is that?" shouted O'Toole.

"Could be the posse we're supposed to be escaping from," Slocum shouted back. But where they had come from was a mystery to him. There seemed to be a dozen horsemen on their tail.

"Slocum! Slocum!" The voice was shouting his name as they pounded out of Red Butte and on down the trail toward the big twin buttes just south of town. He was thankful that he was on a stout little pony, but he wished he had a gun.

Then he heard the voice calling him again. "Slocum! John Slocum! It's Boge Grady. Head for the two buttes, to the right of them. We'll make it out to the ranch!" But was it really Grady?

It was then he realized that while he didn't have his sixgun the owner of his horse had thoughtfully placed a rifle in the saddle scabbard at his knee.

By now he could feel Felix O'Toole lagging behind, and his own horse was beginning to show signs of fatigue. If the posse paced them—pushing with two or three riders and then slackening off while another two pushed—they were done for. Better to take a stand before his horse played out completely.

"Felix, I'm going over when we hit that clump of willow up yonder. You follow."

He didn't hear what his companion said, but the next

thing he knew he'd thrown himself out of the saddle, his hand gripping the rifle, still holding it firmly as he landed on the hard ground. Then he was rolling and finally he came up behind a short stump of willow.

The riders had all started pulling up, the horses heaving, the men cursing, but he noted to his surprise that there was no firing. Maybe it *was* Grady.

He saw that Felix had dropped off his horse, but there was no sound from him. Maybe the little man was knocked out. He could have had a bad fall, for clearly he was no experienced rider.

"Slocum! It's Boge Grady. Don't shoot!" The big horse with its rider was standing only yards away, the animal shaking its head and prancing with the excitement of the chase.

"I've got you covered, mister. Don't make any funny moves!" Slocum's voice cut into the night. And on the instant he had moved. "That goes for any of you," he said from his new position, behind a deadfall. Then he was moving again.

"This is on the level, Slocum. It really is Boge Grady. Kilrain and his deputies are still back in Red Butte. Look, I'm lifting my hands."

Slocum watched as the big man on the big horse raised his arms. "I heard you'd been taken in by Kilrain so I got the boys together. I still want you for that job."

Suddenly Slocum heard the clip-clop of a horse coming fast down the trail.

"You men spread out," the man who had called himself Boge Grady snapped out. "See who it is, damn it!"

To Slocum's astonishment the next voice he heard was a woman's.

"Daddy, it's me. It's Sandra." And these words were followed by tinkling laughter as the rider came into silhouette next to the man on the big horse.

"Sandy, what the devil are you doing out here! You know I've forbidden you to ride at night. It isn't safe. Now get on back to the ranch."

She had ridden her horse right up beside Grady's. With the laughter still in her voice she said, "I'm sorry to have interrupted all your excitement, but I was bored, and I felt like a ride on Sugarhead. Please don't let me interrupt the fun."

Even at the distance he was, Slocum could tell that Grady was furious. "Dan, Bill, escort this young lady back to the main house. Sandy, I am serious!"

The girl silently turned her horse to allow the two riders to escort her back to the ranch.

Slocum stepped out from behind his cover.

"Slocum. I'm Boge Grady."

"I figured that by now. Thanks to the young lady." He was glad to hear the man on the horse let loose a rich chuckle at that.

"By God, Slocum, let's get on back to the outfit. We've got a lot of business to attend to."

"I have to bring my friend along," Slocum said. He called out, "Felix. You still with us?"

"Indeed I am, Slocum. Right now I wouldn't be anywhere else."

Under the evening star Slocum, Felix O'Toole, and Bogardus Grady and his men rode swiftly toward the Double Box ranch. Slocum would have preferred riding with the girl with the laughing, musical voice, but she had gone on ahead with the two riders her father had chosen for her escort. At any rate, he reflected, there was tomorrow. He wondered how Miss Grady would look in the daylight. Anyone with a purring voice like that sure couldn't look bad.

• • •

Boge Grady was known as a man not to be argued with, known all over the Panhandle in the old days as a man who didn't give a good or a bad goddamn about anyone. He stood in the middle of the big room chewing on a wooden lucifer, switching it from one side of his mouth to the other with his eyes on John Slocum. Grady was a big man, heavyset. He'd fought the Kiowa, the Comanches, the Sioux. Sixty going on seventy. His face was leathery and his hands matched. Leather all the way through. His nose was long and he often rubbed it with the back of his gnarled thumb.

"Kilrain now, he was trying to pin the wagon train on you, which he could've done easy if you'd been killed trying to escape. Simple."

"Smart," Slocum said, accepting the havana cigar Boge Grady offered him.

He knew about Grady, had heard of him. There were still men around like Grady, the men who carved their empires out of the land. They had all fought the red man, they had all fought the sodbusters, the sheepmen, even the law, and for sure the outlaws. Anyone and anything that stood in the way of their cattle, their unique way of life that they had created from fighting the land, the Indians, the elements. Bogardus Grady was one of these men who did not earn board and found in a cowboy saddle. These were the big cattle kings. But those days were passing. Grady knew, they all knew, and Bogardus Grady better than most. Slocum was thinking about this as he looked across at the big man turning the cigar thoughtfully in his thick fingers.

Since the great Die-up when the herds had starved and frozen to death, men like Boge Grady had lived with a savage memory. Their eyes turned bleak at the thought or mention of the frozen beeves piled high against fences, the gaunt beasts wandering into towns and eating garbage and the tarpaper from the roofs of houses. And that frightful spring breakup with the rivers way out of their banks, raging torrents of mud and great grinding blocks of ice and the countless carcasses of cattle, with the overall loss in Wyoming alone at fifty percent.

Sure the range had been overstocked, but it was the terrible blizzard with the ground under iron-hard ice so no steer or bull or cow could paw through for feed that had really brought death to the great beef bonanza.

The weather had beaten them then, and there was nothing a man could do about that. Yes, Grady had lost. But he was still here. The ranch was reduced; he didn't have the hands he used to have, only a few now, but he was managing. Down to taking a contract from the army for remounts. It gravelled him, that. By God! A man such as he had been—still was—chasing horses. Not that it wasn't honorable work. But in the old days, mustanging was something you did on the side. Now he was scrambling to keep level. Well, he would never give up.

"I need a man like yourself, knows hosses," he was saying now to John Slocum. "Mostly a man who knows men."

"I smell a difficulty, Grady."

The big man's heavy gray eyebrows shot up, his forehead disappearing in layers of wrinkles. His eyes narrowed, but they were not unfriendly. Slocum had early on noticed that Grady wasn't packing a sidearm. And he knew why.

"How so?" the big man said.

"Like you must have yourself an up-and-up deal with

the army. You know horses, and men, and you've likely
got a crew of fair-to-good hands. Likely some good
Bronc stompers in the bunch. So there's got to be something extra, something rubbing you, is how I see it. Else
why want me?"

"That is so." The rancher nodded. "What you say is
the facts. I have got men, some of them fair seasoned,
some, I got to allow, not so. And I have got . . .
Clifford," he added, with a slight pause before saying
the name.

"Clifford?" Slocum didn't know the name, but he
wondered if Grady was expecting him to.

"Sonny Clifford." Slocum caught the sour strain in
the rancher's voice as he repeated.

Then he remembered something. "Didn't he used to
be—or maybe still is—a range detective?"

Boge Grady nodded heavily and drew on his cigar,
his eyes narrow.

Slocum was trying to remember something he'd
heard about Sonny Clifford, something about a man
who had more questions attached to his reputation than
anyone could come up with answers for. The thought
entered his mind that in the old days, the days of his
former glory, a man like Boge Grady wouldn't worry
over such a man, probably wouldn't even have him
around. And then the thought occurred to Slocum that
maybe it was the girl, Boge's daughter. Maybe it was
the girl Sandy, and Clifford.

"Like you to handle the gather and the working of the
animals both," Grady said. "I know you for a top hand,
and I'll pay top wages and a bonus."

"And the men?"

Grady let a long sigh push through his heavy body.

He squinted at Slocum, canting his head for a tight look. "Them too. That's also why I wrote you. I know you can handle the men."

"You still haven't told me the problem. There are a lot of men can run in wild horses and bust 'em and top them out, and handle a crew of men. You've got something else."

The rancher stood up. Standing, he almost touched the chandelier with the crown of his stetson hat. Without a word he crossed the big room to a roll-top desk, bent down and opened a small cupboard, and brought out a bottle of whiskey. Still without speaking he picked up two glasses from a table at the side of the room and carried them back to where he had been standing with Slocum. He didn't offer the drink, he simply poured. Slocum, for his part, fully appreciated the rancher's movements.

"I see you're a man of few words," he said, offering to lighten it some.

"And I'm told by my family that I use them few more less than more," Grady said, and broke suddenly into a chuckle.

It was a good opening as they both raised their glasses in a toast.

"To the mustangs," Grady said.

A brief silence fell then while Grady collected what he was going to say.

"A while back we ran some broomtails in through Spit Creek, down through this narrow canyon. We was aimin' for our corral in one of the box canyons down by Tensleep. It was a good place. We'd run the hosses in there before, it was a natural. No trouble. But suddenly we seen we'd run ourselves right into a goddamn ambush. I mean, they were crossfiring us thicker'n bees and skeeters. Wounded one of my men, though not bad; creased a couple of horses. The point is, they broke up the gather. We were lucky to get out of there alive." He wagged his big head, his face dark. "The sons of bitches!"

"Any idea who it was?"

"Sure! Ideas? Sure! But no proof on it."

"But you suspicion somebody."

"You bet your ass I do."

"Who?"

"I want you to tell me." Boge Grady reached again for his glass, and sat down holding it, leaning forward in his big chair with his eyes fully on Slocum. "I know who I would bet my bottom dollar on. But I don't want to suspicion you one way or the other. Why I wrote you—another reason—so you can come at it fresh."

Slocum nodded appreciatively at the way Grady was looking at the situation.

"Good enough," he said at last.

Suddenly a grin swept over Boge Grady's leathery face. It seemed almost to burn him. His eyes were very blue, almost watery. He chuckled deep in his chest.

"I would've liked to worked with you in the old days, Slocum."

Slocum nodded. "You can work with me now," he said.

"These here dudes coming out with the cattle companies and all that, they ain't much account. I mean a man can't make a hand out of a one of 'em."

Slocum held up his glass for a toast. "Here's to us," he said. "There are few like us, and damn few like us."

Bogardus Grady broke into a great laugh, shaking his head and shoulders like a feisty buffalo.

It was a good moment as Slocum got up to leave.

The two men stood there in the light of the coal-oil lamps.

"You got that room off the bunkhouse in the little cabin this side," Grady said.

"Good enough. I see you brought my horses from the livery."

"You need anything, holler."

"One thing," Slocum said with his hand on the edge of the door, turning back toward the rancher.

Boge Grady pursed his lips, waiting.

"Where was Sonny Clifford at the time you ran those mustangs and got shot up?"

"Why, back here. Back at the outfit. Far as I know. He had something to do here, I recollect." He looked suspiciously now at Slocum. "Why? What are you thinking?"

"Just wondering. Give it some thought. Maybe you'll remember something."

With a brisk nod, Slocum turned and went out the door.

4

Slocum had decided to ride out and take a look at some
of the wild horses Grady was planning to run in. The
rancher had told him especially about the big buckskin
stallion who ran the biggest herd. But there were a couple of smaller herds, and Slocum felt he wanted to fa-
miliarize himself with the terrain before he risked any
confrontation with whoever was trying to put a crimp
into Boge Grady's horse hunt.

Felix O'Toole had begged to go along with him, and
Slocum didn't feel he could refuse. There was something touching about the little moon-faced man, he carried a sort of dignity that many bigger, surer men didn't.

"Thought we'd try running in a few," he said to Felix
and the three men he'd had brought along from Grady's
crew. "Might be we'll flush up some trouble and get the
real lay of the land."

"I reckon trouble is what we're going to find from here on in," a tall, rangy man said as he sat his steel-dust gelding and built himself a smoke.

"We'll go easy on the shooting. Don't any of you do any shooting unless I tell you."

They rode out early, circling down into the flat land on the other side of the mountain. Slocum's spotted pony was feeling fine and made the other horses strain to keep up with his stride. They saw nothing that first day, but the day after they spotted fresh sign. On the following day they jumped a band of some forty head.

They flushed out of a thicket like birds in flight. An old blaze-faced gray mare was in the lead, and a straw-berry stallion drove them toward the mountains. Once the stud stopped to look back at them.

"They haven't spooked much," Slocum said to one of Grady's men, an oldster with a drop of water hanging off the end of his long nose. He answered to the name of Slim.

"They won't go far," Slim said. "We could get a better look at them tomorrer. There's a handy box canyon yonder could serve us."

The box canyon was of a type characteristic in the Rockies. Natural rock cliffs made walls on three sides, while leaving a grassy floor with water in it. A good feeding area, and simple to hold the horse; a perfect corral when any sort of sensible closure was maintained at the open end. This one was more than a mile long. Slocum stationed Felix and a man named Denton below at the opening, with a backup rider named Cassidy. Slim, meanwhile, kept behind the horses with Slocum hazing them toward the canyon. They didn't have a lot of fight in them and went easily enough. Slocum figured they hadn't been chased much before.

It was about noon when Slocum climbed to the top of a big bronze cliff on the north side of the box canyon, where he could look down at the band of horses without riding in close and disturbing them. He wanted to get a good look at the quality of the horseflesh. Boge Grady had told him he wanted only the best. One good thing, he told himself, they probably wouldn't quit their range, not for a while. He could find them again easily enough.

He lay on his stomach looking through the glasses at the horses below him. He recalled some of the stories he'd heard from old-timers about the Indians walking mustangs down on foot. The Indians would just keep after the horses, packing along their own feed in a sack to keep themselves going, and they would always be there with the horses day and night, never giving them a chance to stop to rest or feed. They kept the herd moving till they got so tired they were easy enough to steer into a trap. Yes, it was a real pleasure looking at those fine, clean animals down below.

Then all at once, totally unexpectedly, it happened. The sharp, unmistakable bark of a repeating rifle snapping through the canyon. And, immediately following, the terrified scream of one of the horses. Instantly the herd was thrown into a frenzy and began charging toward the opening of the box canyon. There were more screams as other rifles opened up.

Slocum hoped to God Grady's men were not firing back. It was evidently what somebody wanted, a fight. He couldn't see whether any horses were down. Maybe they were only spooking them. But it seemed sure they were also trying to bait Grady's men into retaliation.

Automatically he had brought his own rifle up over a rock that was waist-high, but he checked himself. He could see more puffs of smoke about three hundred yards away from where he was positioned, and he heard a repeater cough again. The horses were rearing, kicking, whinnying.

He counted rifle smoke from eight different points on the south rim of the canyon. It would be an easy shot at three hundred yards, but good sense kept his finger off the trigger. It was clear that the five of them were outnumbered.

They shot several more times, not hitting any of the horses. Suddenly the animals broke out of the canyon. Slim and the others had either been driven off by the riflemen or had simply let the herd come through.

And then they were gone. The horses were gone, the men with the rifles were gone. They had disappeared. Slocum scouted the area around him, covering more than a mile. When he got up to higher ground he saw them as moving dots in the distance, their dirty work was done. He counted twelve unknown men. But he would find out who they were. There was no doubt in his mind about that.

Looking down into the canyon he saw Felix O'Toole and Grady's men climbing up to where he was. A dead white horse lay on the floor of the canyon; it looked very white on the new grass.

"You have got to learn to keep under cover better," Slocum told Felix O'Toole. He had sent Grady's three riders on back to the Double Box to report, planning to take some time to scout the area where the riflemen had been. He had found horse tracks and shells, but nothing really useful.

"Want to tell you what I saw." The little man followed Slocum about in disarray. His little round belly was thumping, his moonlike face was flushed, he was sweating, and one hand kept fluttering about like a bird, touching his face, his belt, scratching his crotch, his rear end, tapping the corner of his mouth.

"Yeah, what?"

"I saw one of them fellers up pretty close."

"You're lucky he didn't see you."

"Had a scar down the left side of his face. Mean-looking. Real mean. I mean, *mean!*" He closed his little eyes and shook his head.

"Huh."

"You gonna foller them?"

"Not much sense in that since you know what they look like, and I know pretty much what they were riding. They'll be about."

"Slocum . . ."

Slocum turned his head to study the man standing beside him. There was something extra in his voice.

"I was a mite scared down there, being that close to those men."

Suddenly Slocum felt the smile taking over his face. He liked Felix O'Toole. "I'd have been scared too, I reckon."

They stood on the floor of the box canyon now, studying the horse droppings, the churned-up grass. All the horses but one were gone. The white mare lay on her side. She had been shot through the head.

As they rode now with their horses kicking up little plumes of dust in the heat of the day, Slocum tried piecing it together. Who were the horse killers? Grady had put it that somebody else was hunting horses, but had not mentioned a name. Was it someone who wanted the horses, or wanted to get Boge Grady?

They drew rein at the bank of a little creek and sat their horses.

"We'll breathe 'em a spell," Slocum said. After a minute he dismounted.

His companion let out a long, weary sigh, and dropped painfully down from his saddle. "This cowboy life is not for me, Slocum."

Slocum grinned. "You're doing all right."

"Maybe." Felix O'Toole shrugged. "Maybe better'n being in that damn jail."

"What were you in for?"

"A trumped-up charge."

"That is just exactly what I figured, you know that?" Slocum's tone was dry as a lemon. He winked slyly at Felix O'Toole. "Got you on your money-making, huh?"

"That was the real reason. Not what I'd been doing, but the sheriff wanted me to make him some money for free."

"Our noble sheriff, huh?"

Felix O'Toole's head nodded so sharply that his derby hat almost fell off. He adjusted it quickly. "Sheriff Kilrain allowed as how he was interested in engaging my special talents for creating fresh, beautiful, and wholly authentic coins. Notably those ten-dollar gold eagles you have already seen." He sniffed. "And I have got other suspicions for you, mister, if you are interested."

"Don't give me that coy stuff, give it to me straight. Was it Kilrain after those horses out at the canyon? His men, I mean."

Felix O'Toole's eyes opened wide. He scratched his stomach. "How did you know that? I only overheard a word or two, and his name was mentioned."

"Easy enough figuring why he tried to railroad me into blame on that wagon train. He knew I was connected somehow with Boge Grady. And Grady is horses. Got it? The sheriff is onto running horses himself, or he's simply out to bust Grady for some other reason we don't know about. Could be both. I'll bet on the horses. There's money in that, and it's safer than his present business."

"His present business? You mean being sheriff, and all that?"

"I don't mean being sheriff, I mean being 'all that,' as you say."

Felix O'Toole's eyes almost bugged out of their sockets at that, and he was speechless. A moment passed, then another. Finally he said, "Where does that leave us?"

"It leaves us right here," Slocum said. "You get on back to Grady's. Better be careful if you go into town, with Kilrain on the path. He'll still want to corral us, and maybe even worse."

"And you? Where are you going?" The little man's voice rose in alarm as he swiftly took off his derby hat and then put it back on again.

"I'm going to do some more looking around."

"Take me with you."

"I don't want company. Besides, you've got to figure a way to get hold of your tools and equipment and get back to work."

"I figured I might be helping you, Slocum, especially since I can't go into town. I can tag along, and I won't talk."

Slocum had stepped into his saddle stirrup and swung up onto the spotted horse. "You can help me by keeping your eye on somebody," he told Felix.

"Sure will." His companion brightened immediately.
"Who would that be?"

"A young woman; tall, dark. She hangs out at the
Broken Dollar, I have been told. But she might also
come around the Double Box, since she does enjoy
business. And you just might be able to wangle into
town now and again if the sheriff or his deputies aren't
about. They're not exactly a vigilante bunch as far as
upholding the law. You might have a chance. Just a
thought."

"What do you want me to see?" O'Toole asked,
frowning.

"See if she sees the sheriff or maybe Big Jaw or
Grady, or even a man named Sonny Clifford. And let
me know fast."

"When will you be back?"

"Not long." Slocum lifted the reins from his horse's
neck and nodded at Felix O'Toole.

"Slocum, has this person got a name?"

"Yep, she does. Sweetheart Moon is the name she
goes by, I do believe." Touching the brim of his hat in a
friendly gesture, he kicked the spotted pony into a brisk
little canter.

Felix O'Toole didn't kick his horse into anything. He
sat deep in his saddle, his mouth hanging open, his face
wreathed in total dejection. He sat there watching as his
friend rode toward the high benchland to the north.

Nobody knew more poignantly than Felix O'Toole that
one of the most frustrating deficits of many western
towns was the great female shortage. Indeed, it was just
this problem that had driven Felix to accelerate the out-
put of his merchandise and so had attracted the attention
of Sheriff Lupis Kilrain. But he really wasn't worried

about the law. Felix was a realist and understood that the men of the law were in business too, that they too had to make a living, and that they too yearned for the sweet fruits that money could buy. The point was, Felix O'Toole understood fully how much his talent was needed. In a sense, it gave him more protection than half a dozen guns or gunmen.

It was at Pitcherville that his budding talent for counterfeiting received the initial boost it needed. At Pitcherville he had first set eyes on a large, heavily bosomed, big-handed lady named Big Kate. This was in the Happy Times Drinking and Gaming Emporium.

Kate was just an inch less than six feet and she looked quite down at Felix O'Toole's five feet five inches. She was about to send him packing when he had offered to buy her a drink, but suddenly she noticed the large diamond he was wearing on one of his little fingers.

"Don't mind if I do," she'd said nobly, and smoothed her copious bosom with her large hands, letting her palms roam all the way down her belly and over her hips and buttocks. Felix O'Toole was mightily impressed.

And Big Kate was impressed at the way her new companion paid for the drinks with a golden flourish of eagles, solid coin.

She smiled on Felix, who had just spent four womanless years in prison. "Honey, for a hundred dollars I can give you a good time. I am expensive, but you'll see why. And the higher you want to go, the better it gets."

"Please do not consider money a problem," Felix had said firmly as he reached again to his purse. "Let's try a hundred for openers."

With his ten-dollar mold die, a small charcoal stove, and several copper ingots—all portable on horseback—Felix began knocking out the coins. In no time at all he could pour five hundred, say. These he plated with a thin layer of an alloy of which nine parts were gold and one part was silver-copper. This happened to be the ratio used by the U.S. Mint in the manufacture of bona fide money. The finished product looked, weighed, and even sounded like the government coins. These he sold at half price, that is to say, at five dollars each, but in lots of five hundred. There were likely places for this transaction—the saloons, where it was easy to pass counterfeit money, the dance halls, amongst miners on payday, and with the sporting girls. Some saloonkeepers bought as many as a thousand counterfeit eagles at a shot, to the tune of $5,000. Both the recipient and the creator of this product garnered a tidy profit.

Thus had Felix wooed Big Kate and won her. They moved in together and set up housekeeping. Big Kate retired from her career and Felix expanded his.

But, alas, the leopard does not change its spots, and it wasn't long before Felix discovered that his love was back in business. Driven into a fury of jealousy, Felix roused himself to such a pitch that he beat her with a singletree and nearly killed her.

The citizens of the town were enraged, the woman shortage being so critical, and Felix was very nearly lynched. Fortunately his talent for making money was remembered and he was allowed to escape the wrath of the male populace. With the tools of his trade on a packhorse, and riding a sorrowful-looking crowbait, he roamed the countryside, picking up business here and there. At last he found himself in Red Butte, and one evening as he paid for his drinks and played the wheel of fortune with his fabulous golden eagles at the Broken Dollar a voice purred in his direction and he smelled the odor of musk.

"That sure is pretty-looking money you've got there," the voice said, caressing Felix over his entire body and especially between his legs. He was facing a beauty of no mean proportion. This was no Big Kate, but a woman who displayed every curve and wiggle known to man.

"Can I buy you a drink?" Felix said, hardly able to believe he wasn't dreaming the beauty who stood before him in a slinky red satin gown which seemed to be held up only by the prominence and spring of her fantastic breasts.

"I would be delighted, honey. What's your name?"

Felix beamed as he told her his name. "What's your name, lady?" He was almost stammering with excitement.

The purring voice deepened as the two velvet eyes fell over the bridge of his nose, dropping down to his mouth. "Just call me Sweetheart. Sweetheart Moon's my name."

By God, he was thinking now as he rode his pony toward Boge Grady's Double Box ranch, *by God.* And he felt himself gray and cold inside and out, hearing like a knell the words of John Slocum to watch her—the love of his life.

Was it his fate to be taken by such women? Felix had had few women in his life, but it seemed that every damn one of them was the same as the last—untrustworthy. And yet, Sweetheart Moon—maybe because she was the latest, he realized, being a philosopher—

was the best, the one who attracted him the most. His heart began to beat more rapidly as he thought of her out there on the trail.

And what the hell, he was thinking, *if she is, she is, and if she ain't, then she ain't.* He knew he shouldn't have crazy illusions about Sweetheart, shouldn't let himself get all twisted up the way he had about Big Kate; but then, he also knew that he wanted to.

Being a practical person at heart, Felix manfully turned his attention to his enterprise, figuring out mentally as he rode along just how many golden eagles he could get out in the next day or two.

Slocum still wasn't satisfied. He'd certainly got hold of the flavor of the business at hand: the determination of Lupis Kilrain to go to any lengths to stop Grady's horse hunt. But there was still the wish to see the big buckskin stallion and his particular herd. It was a feeling, and he had felt it in Grady when they'd spoken back at the Double Box. Sure, there were hundreds of other horses, but the buckskin apparently had eluded capture for the longest time. "No question, he is special," Grady had said. "And I want him!"

And then too, Slocum wanted to be alone. He was glad to be rid of the three Double Box men. They were competent, and that was about all. Alone he felt free, free to roam and think and figure out how he would go about the horse hunt, and how he would handle Lupis Kilrain and his gang of killers. Kilrain, it was clear, was playing for keeps.

Judging from the position of the sun, he reckoned he'd have plenty of time to look at the other side of the high benchland. And as he rode on, he began to think about Kilrain and the wagon train. The fact that the sheriff had been so almighty eager to pin it on him in some way clearly showed he was covering up something. And then he had known that he, Slocum, would be working with Grady. Was there something going on between the two of them—Grady and Kilrain—that was bigger than the horse hunt?

Topping the lip of a long draw now and looking down a great sweep of fresh buffalo grass, he saw two riders. They were sitting their horses near a stand of cottonwood trees that lined a creek. One was a woman, as near as he could judge.

Not wishing to be seen, he cut back down under the edge of the draw and followed a trail into some thick spruce and pine. A while later when he emerged farther down and nearer the creek and the cottonwoods he saw that the riders were still in the same place. They were evidently involved in an intense conversation, but they wouldn't have seen him anyway, since he was still keeping under cover just inside a thin line of willows.

He sat his horse, watching them. The woman was young, and he could tell by the way she moved that she was spirited. The man was young too, but stolid. He sat his big sorrel horse arrogantly. Judging by the horseflesh they were riding they were not from the down side of town. The sorrel with the four white stockings was a sound horse, a good fifteen hands, and the man sat him like an English rider. He was no cowpoke. The girl's chestnut was a chunky animal, and tough-looking. Slocum would have picked the chestnut for endurance, the sorrel for a short race.

Suddenly Slocum wondered if the girl was Sandy Grady. He'd not seen her that evening when she'd encountered Boge and his riders in the deep twilight, but he'd heard her voice. And while he couldn't hear her from where he was right now, there was something in the proud way she sat the chestnut that gave him the feeling it was she. But who would the man be? Sonny Clifford? The name popped into his thoughts from nowhere.

It must be so. She was obviously an expensive young lady. Something of the lilt in her voice the other night had told him that—rich, spoiled, willful. But now, watching her back, still protected by the trees, he felt her anger bristling through her body. The man was raising his voice, but Slocum still couldn't distinguish any words. He was angry too; his gestures clearly showed it. By contrast, the girl's anger was controlled. There was something about the way she was handling her companion that struck Slocum forcibly. And he realized again how much more expressive the human body was than actual words. Yes, she was right in herself. And he liked that quality in a woman.

He didn't want to watch any more; he didn't want to spy. He turned his pony's head and began moving back through the trees to pick up the trail farther along the creek and well away from the interesting young lady and her irate companion.

When he saw her again, a good hour later, she was alone, working her little chestnut horse up a narrow trail toward the high rocks from where Slocum had just spotted a herd of wild mustangs in the near distance.

He had watched them for several moments grazing peacefully. And then all at once there was the big stallion, the buckskin. His lion-colored coat glistened in the late afternoon sun as he moved amongst his mares, shaking his great black mane, swishing his black tail, then suddenly stopping, head raised, neck arched, as he listened. Slocum had felt his breath catch. It was a magnificent sight. He had just turned away, for no particular reason—he attributed it later to his extra sense—and had seen the girl coming along the trail he had recently traveled.

She was surprised to find somebody there at the top of the rise. And Slocum looked at her quite openly. She was beautiful, with dark brown hair, dark brown eyes, creamy skin, and a figure under her lime-colored silk riding shirt and extremely tight breeches that brought him to instant excitement. When she pulled up the reins to bring the chestnut to a stop he caught the quiver of her breasts under the green silk.

"John Slocum's the name, miss." He touched the brim of his Stetson hat.

"Yes, I know, Mr. Slocum. I remember you. I am Sandra Grady."

She had two freckles on her turned-up nose that he found delightful. His eyes moved down to her open collar, and he felt more than actually saw color creeping into her face.

"Do you always inspect people so carefully, Mr. Slocum?"

"Only special people, Miss Grady."

"I see." But she didn't move. Then she said, "I'm actually looking for some wild horses. I understand from my father that there are a few herds about."

"Well, you've come to the right party, miss. I've just spotted a fine herd, with a stallion anyone would give half their life for."

Her eyes lit up immediately. "Not the buckskin I've been hearing so much about?"

"Come on!" He kicked his pony ahead of hers and started back up to where he had watched the mustangs.

In a few moments they were at the edge of the high

rise of ground looking down into the sweeping valley where more than a hundred head of horses were grazing.

"There he is!" Her voice was trembling with excitement as she adjusted her field glasses.

Slocum already had his trained on the magnificent animal. "Daddy says the stallion bosses the whole bunch."

"He sure does."

"That must be a sight to see." She lowered the glasses, her eyes still on the horses below.

Slocum watched a wisp of brown hair blowing lightly on her forehead.

"I want to come along when you run them in. It must be so exciting."

He began to tell her about some of the smart stallions he'd seen bossing bands of horses and how, when the stud felt there was danger, he'd charge right smack through the herd, scattering the mares so they couldn't get caught all bunched together.

He told her how a stud drives his band out of trouble, with one of the old mares getting in front, the stud behind, biting and kicking, driving and turning the horses. The stallion might get in front to lead them when they were going for water or when he didn't know where there might be trouble coming, but the minute he knew where the danger was he'd get behind and drive them for all they were worth.

The buckskin had stopped feeding and now again stood stock-still, his head raised, ears pointing forward and up, his eyes large and questioning. Every inch of his magnificent body was alert. The muscles under the tawny skin were still, and yet alive with silent movement. It wasn't something you could see, but feel. Slocum pointed it out to the girl.

"Yes, yes, I understand. You can feel his—his power!" she said, and sucked in her breath.

Suddenly the buckskin let out a scream. Wheeling almost a half circle, he charged right through the center of the feeding horses, kicking them, biting, still screaming out his call of danger. His ears were flat down on his great neck as his great teeth slashed here and there. The horses were racing out of the meadow, tails and manes flying in the wind created by their own haste to get to safety. And in only a few moments they were gone, leaving only their smell. The meadow was silent.

Slocum saw the tears standing in her eyes. He could still feel the excitement of the mustangs all through his body. Now it was blending with his excitement for the girl beside him.

"Come on," he said. "It'll be getting dark soon."

She turned toward her horse and with her hand up on the saddlehorn she turned to look at him. "Mr. Slocum, you do surprise me."

He was already up on his horse, wrapping his hand in the reins and mane together. "I hope it's pleasant, miss."

She didn't answer, but turned and put her foot into her stirrup and mounted. His eyes followed the smooth, round, full shape of her buttocks, and he felt his erection driving against his trousers.

In her saddle she looked at him again. "You surprise me," she repeated. "I must say I had expected you to try to make love to me."

Slocum canted his head at her, squinting a little as though looking at something strange. "Miss, first of all, wait till you're asked. And, secondly, when I take the notion, I won't *try* to make love to you."

Holding his eyes on her long enough to see the color coming into her face, he kicked the spotted pony and started back down the trail.

The evening had just dropped down on the land as they rode into the Double Box ranch.

5

The sheriff of Red Butte and environs, including Mile City, ruled an area that took days to ride over no matter in which direction you went. Sheriff Lupis Kilrain was standing at the window of his office when the knock came. He continued to stand stock-still, hard as a gun barrel, a cold cigar butt clamped in his bony jaws. He was looking out toward the south, beyond that area nearest his window which was known as the Gold Coast, and for which Red Butte had acquired a certain fame.

Lupis Kilrain did not reply to the knock. He didn't speak. He didn't move a muscle. The knock came again, louder, and he remained as he was. A statue of anger defying patience. He listened to the door open behind him, heard the wet intake of breath at the surprise his presence called in the two men who entered.

He didn't have to look. He knew them, had been expecting them, had been waiting. Patiently waiting. For Clyde Dancey and Big Jaw Turk Nosniffer.

"Sheriff . . ." Big Jaw brought the word from somewhere high in his throat.

Lupis Kilrain remained silent, a stone staring out the window. Actually, he was thinking suddenly of Sweetheart Moon, wondering where she was. As always when his thoughts turned to this particular lady, he wondered if she was alone. Any thought of her duplicity was always difficult for him to bear. He regretted having used her to set up Slocum, yet she had sworn that the man hadn't touched her.

"Sheriff, we just got back from Maundry Canyon," Dancey said. "Run into Slocum but he didn't see us. We bust up his roundup."

"Like to tell you on what happened," Big Jaw put in, the words coming out thick and wet, for he was chewing a big wad of tobacco.

Suddenly, like a whip, the sheriff spun to face them. He watched their faces fall as they met his laughing eyes. Lupis Kilrain knew they were afraid of him; it was the way he liked it. Keep the buggers off balance—everybody, for the matter of that. Keep them guessing. Fun them. Order them. Humiliate and browbeat them. Give them nothing. "Trust nobody and you'll know who betrayed you" was the motto. He wished he could trust Sweetheart Moon.

"I know you're back," he snapped, his voice sounding like it was half-buried in gravel. "I already got word on what happened." Then, without any warning, he shouted at the top of his lungs, "You goddamned fools! What the hell do you think you're doing out there, shooting horses! You assholes!"

They stood there, the two of them, looking down, then stealing careful looks at their employer, not daring to look directly into those gleaming "laughers."

"You want to turn the whole country against you, against me! Is that it! You're out to get me hung! You idiots!"

"We couldn't help it, Lupis," Dancey said, having more grip on himself than Big Jaw and so using a modest familiarity. "We wuz trying to bust them animals out of that canyon where they run 'em, and Hendricks elevated too low on one of them mares. Trying to scare her."

"A nice little white mare," Big Jaw said, nodding his large oblong head vigorously.

Lupis Kilrain's eyes popped. "Scare her! With a rifle! Christ!" He couldn't contain it; he was almost choking at the stupidity of his subordinates. "For Christ's sake, don't you knotheads know nothin'? You need a rifle to scare a wild, unbroke hoss! By God, I work my fingers to the nubs, work my brain till I'm like filled with sand, dead on my feet; nights, days, planning the Plan, working it all out. We got the Territory at our feet. You fools! We got the miners coming and going. The drummers, travelers, everybody. There ain't a stage going or coming in the Territory we don't have marked for the organization. We got the law! Me! *I* am the law! Look at McCone's wagons! Worked like a clock. I mean, except for that son of a bitch stumbling onto it. I told you assholes to keep a sharper eye on the place, even clean it up. You're lucky Slocum came by there so we can tell it is him done it. But no thanks to you fools!" He stopped, exhausted, coughing, bringing up phlegm, old tobacco, and more heavy cursing.

"But then . . ." He had found his voice again. "Then

we had it set up for his escape, and that little guy who makes the money. But Slocum I'm talking about; I fixed it so we'd bugger Grady and pin the wagon train on Slocum all at the same time. It was all set, easy as a cat licking his own ass. But that got fucked up! You fucked that up! Can't you stupid, buggered bastards do anything like I tell you!"

"We can still get him," Big Jaw said after a brief pause, hoping to soften the wrath that was all but bringing the two of them to their knees.

"Oh, we'll get him," snapped Kilrain. "We will get him. No doubt there. But it will no doubt have to be me takes it on myself in person. Because, by God, there will be no more mistakes. We are aiming too high for any more fucking up! But we won't arrest him. Mind! Leave him free—for now."

"Right, chief," Dancey said. "I'll get that son of a bitch!"

"When I tell you. You both mind that!"

"Right." Big Jaw nodded.

"No more dumb things." The voice was softer.

"Like with Sweetheart, you mean?" Big Jaw said. "In the hotel room."

It was the wrong thing to say. Both Dancey and Big Jaw saw that instantly. But it was too late. They braced themselves for the molten lava that would be heaped upon them. But what came was worse.

Lupis Kilrain was silent. He had become ice, frozen into a monument of venom. After some moments his lips began to move stiffly. For a few sentences they couldn't hear him. But his voice began to rise.

"Do not mention that episode again. Ever. EVER!" His last word was screamed out of his burning throat. Panting, he fell again to coughing. "Shit take it!

Rheumy again, damn it!" For several moments he was helpless under the wracking cough that had seized him. Slowly he began to recover. He was sweating. He took off his hat; he mopped his brow.

"Now listen." The voice was calm, controlled. "Listen to me carefully. Get Gilhooley and Ramirez."

"They're over to Horsehead," Big Jaw said.

Lupis Kilrain looked toward the ceiling. "I did not ask you where they were. I told you to get them and bring them here."

Big Jaw nodded.

The patience of centuries was in the sheriff's voice now as he spoke. "Do you think you can do that?"

"Consider it done, boss."

"Christ!" The word came softly, just on the breath— a prayer.

There followed a moment of silence. Lupis Kilrain had turned to the window. "Send me Ramirez and Gilhooley."

He heard the door close behind them, in the reflection of the window glass saw that it was shut. Then he turned back into the room, walked over to his desk, and sat down.

Pierre, the brindle-colored cat, lying in the sunlight, lifted his head to look over with supreme indolence. Then with a couple of swift shakes of his head he rolled over and turned his back to the man, stretched on his side, then lay still.

"Go to hell," said Lupis Kilrain with a disdainful glance at the animal. He reached into one of the desk drawers and took out a fresh cigar. It was very dry; the wrapper was beginning to flake off. He dropped spittle on it and rubbed the whole barrel of the cigar, including the ends. He began working it with his fingers. It wasn't

as dry as he had thought at first. Good enough. He
struck a lucifer and lit up. The sharp blue smoke cut into
his small office and he sat back in his chair, crossing his
right ankle over his knee, and let his thoughts run over
his plan.

It had all started so simply, those months ago, not
long after he'd ridden into Red Butte, neatly dodging
the law back in Idaho. The thing was, no one in Red
Butte knew anything about him. He was clean. What
was more, he could play the role of affability, courtli-
ness, the respectable gambler awaiting the right business opportunity. He was knowledgeable about mining,
stock, horses, and guns, and at the same time an able
conversationalist with respectable ladies. He was, fur-
thermore, a good looking man, and he knew it. But the
women were few in town, and those who were considered respectable were already spoken for. Lupis Kilrain
didn't mind. He in fact preferred the livelier ladies, and
spent his time with the soiled doves.

It was in that quarter of town known as the Gold
Coast that he had encountered Sweetheart Moon. Had
fallen immediately for her undeniable charms. Nor did
Lupis have any difficulties in outdistancing rivals.
Moreover, Sweetheart appeared to return his favors with
equal passion.

Yet he yearned for respectability. Somehow the
honors that contemporaries could confer upon a man
had always eluded him. Since early boyhood his life had
been a series of scrapes, dubious encounters, disasters
from which either God or the Devil had rescued him, or
at any rate had arranged it so that he could rescue himself. Thus, in California he had escaped jail, in Colo-
rado a tar-and-feathering, in Idaho a hanging. There had

been duped husbands, vengeful wives, slickered card mechanics. Other, less violent episodes had filled in the gaps. None of these happenings contributed toward the respectability for which he yearned.

The office of sheriff offered what he was looking for. It was not an office carrying high remuneration, but it was absolutely fixed in the social scale. People looked up to a sheriff. Small boys ran after you in the street, begging stories of high action and drama. He was invited into homes; people asked his advice. And it was, moreover, an obvious stepping stone to higher levels. Lupis Kilrain saw all this with remarkable clarity. There was only one thing in his way in this new, growing town of Red Butte, and that was the present incumbent. Red Butte already had a sheriff; solid, stolid, dull Cyrus Quint. But fortune smiled. Sheriff Quint one fine day up and caught lead poisoning, courtesy of a bullet through the lungs, and expired.

It was Charlie Pfouts who asked Lupis to run for the vacated office. He would always remember that day when his voice, smooth as a pearl, had accepted the offer. Masterfully he had played the role of modesty, love of the law, purity of heart. Anyway, he really did believe in those things. He was not a professional gambler for peanuts.

The campaign was brisk, short, and without any charged incident. Few in town had a doubt as to the outcome. Lupis Kilrain's opponent was a nondescript named Joe Nun, and he was never heard of again. It was only too clear that the handsome gambler was the sensible choice—and, what was more, he was a gambler who was adroit with his gun. Victory was easy.

That evening there was high celebration in the saloons of Red Butte. Everyone felt personally that the new sheriff was his man. The gamblers, the miners, the businessmen, the leaders of the community, each felt that good old Lupis Kilrain represented his interests.

"You sure enough treed the town this day, Lupis." Charlie Pfouts lifted his glass high in the Antelope Saloon. "And I say long life to you."

Lupis still carried the little holiday that had sung in his heart at hearing those words.

Then, without any warning, success was piled on success. At Mile City fresh gold was discovered and a whole new town sprang into existence overnight. The topping on the cake, however, was the fact that Red Butte was still the district center, meaning that whoever was sheriff of Red Butte was also sheriff of Mile City, a fiefdom truly large.

Lupis Kilrain was not naive; he knew that gold also attracts goldseekers of a variety not accustomed to work with pick and shovel. After all, he himself was a member of the fraternity. The new sheriff, attempting to cover an area almost as big as the eastern state of Connecticut, soon discovered the impossibility of his job. In his area there were at least two dozen of the toughest criminals in the West, and scores more toughs, thieves, and whiskeyed miners and cowboys. Lupis Kilrain and his two deputies—Clyde Dancey and only lately Big Jaw Turk Nosniffer—were called to control this veritable guerrilla army.

It wasn't long before the complaints began coming in.

"The citizens are getting fed up, Lupis," was the way Charlie Pfouts put it. "We know you're doing all you can, but, man, it's getting out of hand."

Lupis had told him, "Charlie, last Saturday—hell, I had so many drunks locked up in jail I had to turn 'em away when my deputies brought more in."

"Lupis, we're all with you. We know you've got a helluva job to do here. But something's got to be done."

"I need more deputies. Good ones. Dancey isn't enough."

"I'll get the word around," Pfouts had promised. "But you know better than me how it is. Anyone good with a gun is not to be trusted. And then, too, people don't want to pay for law and order; they just want to have it."

"Sure—for free."

Pfouts had unbent a little then. He was a big man, amiable by nature and respected all over town. "Course, Lupis, you do have one big advantage."

The sheriff had replied sardonically that it would be nice to know just what that was.

"The way I see it, the outlaws are not all that organized."

"How so?" Kilrain had found his interest touched. Not a few times the same thought had struck him, but he said nothing of this, playing it with total innocence. Also, he wanted to hear Pfouts out.

"I mean," Charlie Pfouts said, "they're all independent of each other. They work here and there, usually at small pickings, which add up, of course. But there's no chief running them. If they ever got themselves organized, the law wouldn't be worth a bottle of cold piss. What I am saying is you're lucky, in a way."

"In a way!" He had grinned wryly, going along with Pfouts.

Of course he knew it. How could he not? Here in

Red Butte and in Mile City, even with the toughs not
organized into a band, the law was holding the thin end
of the stick.

And, by God, hadn't he been hearing it from others,
not just Pfouts!

"Can't you do something, Kilrain?"

"Sheriff, these road agents have got to be stopped!"

"It isn't safe to go out after dark, and even in daylight, Sheriff Kilrain!"

And so on and so on, until he wanted to tell the
whole damn lot of them to go plumb to hell.

And that morning when Horton Wills Foley had ac-
costed him on the street. He had just stepped outside of
his bank; a tall, thin man with a long guttered face and a
nervous cough. "Sheriff, it's got to stop! Killings, robberies. Can't you get some worthwhile deputies?"

True, there had been no direct unfriendliness in the
remark, yet it had cut deep.

He'd replied, "I am doing all that I can, Mr. Foley.
I'm not offering excuses, but with a couple of hundred
toughs and road agents in an area this size with just
myself and one deputy, a deputy not of the highest quality, I must admit . . ." He opened his hands in a gesture
of helplessness to the other man.

The banker had taken a step backward, bowing his
head, holding up a conciliatory palm. "It's all right,
Sheriff. None of us are blaming you. There's nothing
personal in my remarks. It's just that it is really getting
out of hand. A terrible situation! Terrible!" He had
wagged his long head in doleful emphasis.

No, nothing personal. But wasn't there really a sort
of silent criticism? Surely if he were capable he would
be able to handle the outlaw element. Weren't they
thinking that, if not saying it amongst themselves? Sure,

he'd brought some in. The usual drunks he'd already totted up to Charlie Pfouts, and some loudmouthed toughs and petty thieves. But the big road agent jobs, the big robbing of travelers and miners, that was another matter.

Take that last killing at Tensleep; the killer hadn't left a trace. And at Rattlesnake Creek, three miners had been robbed and beaten almost to death. One of them would be lame for life. And the Gebo stage. That had been the worst. Held up just where it was necessary to slow for Horsehead Crossing. Everything stripped, including the passengers. The driver shot dead to boot. He'd gotten up a posse, but the trail was cold, and the men in the posse had little heart for it in sub-zero weather.

Who really cared, when you got right down to it? A few robberies and killings. Who cared all that much when so many riches were so close at hand? Who had the time to go looking for killers and thieves when there was gold to be had for the asking? A man would be crazy to risk his life for pennies—if even that—when thousands of dollars in gold were just lying about.

So what did they expect a man to do? Hell, he could be out getting rich himself instead of chasing after some whiskeyed killer, and risking his life as well. By God, Lupis Kilrain would like to enjoy some of that gold too. So his thoughts had run.

And then one day the light had hit. True, as Pfouts had pointed out, and as he himself had long noted, the outlaws were not organized. But someone was sure to come along some day and do just that. And then watch out!

So why not he? Why not let the law organize them? How about that? And then he, the sheriff, would be in

control of them, would know where they were de-
ployed, would know who and how many they were and
what they intended. He could anticipate their moves. In
short, he could foil them, control them.

Lupis Kilrain would be in full command. A few
small crimes could be permitted, and there could be a
suitable number of arrests. Since he would know everyone's activity, he could keep crime in the Territory to a
minimum. And, most important, he would be in control.

The thought was almost too big. He pondered it,
honed it, spending hours going over details. Yes, a
thought, a plan worthy of his great talent as organizer,
leader. And again he was singing inside.

Such a simple beginning, he was thinking now as he
sat in his office with the late afternoon sunlight playing
across the windowsill and spilling into a pool in which
Pierre, the brindle cat, lay dozing.

Yes, simple. And things had gone well for that first
year. They'd gone well until Boge Grady had decided to
collect men for his wild horse hunt.

Grady had pretty much stayed out of the sheriff's
way, the Double Box being on the other side of Tensleep
and not so much within the sheriff's purview. And
Grady had been working his cattle, trying to get things
going again after a series of setbacks. But Boge Grady
had also been outspoken about the lackadaisical law in
Red Butte and environs. Besides, Grady was respected
in town and especially by the outlying ranchers. He
could be trouble. And he'd been asking people about
Morgan McCone and his wagon train.

The trouble was Lupis had his eye on those horses on
the north of Tensleep. Plenty of wild horse stuff there,
more than a few bunches of tough mustangs. Lupis

needed fresh horses for his organization.

There was always a need for horses. He had to be sure none of the men were traced through their mounts by any private vigilante types—like Boge Grady, who didn't mind taking the law into his own hands. So far the problem had been well handled by painting out any distinctive markings such as white stars or white feet with a cheap paint that could later be washed out with turpentine. For while there were plenty of horses to be had—they could be rented or bought from any stable in town—the trouble was that coach drivers, for instance, had an uncanny ability to identify just about every horse in the country. If the horse was any good, someone had coveted it, and if it wasn't any good, there was no point in getting it.

But the source of horseflesh, the best place for the wild mustangs to be run down and corralled, was beyond the Double Box, far on the north side of Tensleep. And Lupis had been setting it up for himself—in the back of his mind—that horse running would be a good way for him to cover himself. His present operation with the toughs and road agents couldn't go on too long. He'd need another operation, something respectable. He was even now working up a contract with the army, through Harley Glenderson. The only trouble was Grady. Grady was going to be working the same area. And the worst thing was that Grady had John Slocum ramrodding his horse hunt.

Well, by golly, he had a couple of aces to play. He had Gilhooley and Ramirez; and he was sure not signing them on as deputies. They were his private deputies. Yes, Slocum had backwatered them at the Chicago House. But that was to the good. They were both madder than hornets. He could count on them.

But his big ace in the hole was Sonny Clifford. And soon he could ditch the sheriff business and really get respectable.

He smiled to himself, sitting there in the sunlight, thinking of some of the others who were working the roads and trails leading in and out of Red Butte and Mile City, men such as Bill Pitcher, Moss Haines, Whiskey Joe Ching, the Bigger brothers. These were the killers, shooting guards and drivers from ambush and then swooping down on the unprotected coaches. Sometimes the coach teams ran away, out of control, and went plunging to their deaths over steep embankments, dragging coach and passengers with them. But those boys were making it tough for everybody else.

So thick were the road agents that drivers and guards got the jitters and quit. No, it would be time soon now for him to quit.

Still . . . the public reaction to the depredations of the road agents—aside from the brutal killings—was actually one of general satisfaction. Wells, Fargo & Company, by virtue of the stranglehold it kept on transportation, its rough service and its high passenger and freight rates, could expect little sympathy from the public, and got none. As for the robbed passengers, well, they were taking their chances. If they didn't get robbed on the stage, they would somewhere else. All told, the free-spending road agents were regarded as a healthy force that kept money in local circulation instead of letting it escape out of the country.

All well and good. And he had a pretty good spy system, knowing which shipments were going where, and when, and with which drivers and guards. There were occasional slip-ups, but so far nothing disastrous. Only he had to be careful about Grady. Grady had a big mouth, and he had started asking questions, especially since moving in on the horse business.

But now, reflecting on aces in the hole, his thoughts turned to Sweetheart Moon. And all at once there came a knock on the door. Since he'd been thinking of his superb friend, a voice in him suggested that it would be indeed marvelous if that was she.

"Come," he said and swung his body forward in order to be able to greet friend or foe accordingly. He was astounded to be met with that tantalizing odor that excited him beyond any possible understanding.

"I been missing you, honey."

Lupis felt something clutch simultaneously at his throat and his crotch. "Lock the door," he said.

She stood there, tall, her hand on her hip, her breasts thrusting right out at him, her mouth almost speaking to him though her lips were quite still, while slightly parted, as though waiting for something.

"Are you telling me you want it here?" she said.

"Lock it."

With a slow, wicked smile, she turned and locked the door. "Can't you wait till we get to bed, honey?"

He was already reaching over and undressing her, while she knelt and started to unbuckle his belt.

"Where you been?" he said huskily. "What you been doing?"

"Just waiting for you, honey. Just sitting at home thinking about you and that great big thing you got there."

At the window Pierre lifted his head to turn and look at what was going on. Shaking his head rapidly and giving a swift yawn, he turned back to the pleasures of sleep.

· · ·

"So, who you figure?" Boge Grady took the stalk of grass out of his mouth, shifted his weight, and in the late afternoon sunlight canted his head toward John Slocum.

The two men were squatting in the middle of the big round horse corral, with the sun warm on their backs and on the backs of their hands as they discussed the action out at the box canyon.

"Looks like Kilrain, and that's a gut," Slocum said drily. "O'Toole was up close enough to shake hands with a couple of the men, one with a long scar down his face, and he heard Kilrain's name."

"That'd be Cooly Dunrud, I'd reckon. He is no man to get previous with. The others?" He squinted up at the sky from beneath the brim of his big Stetson hat, remarking the weather for the morrow as he spoke.

"He didn't see them."

"You trust that feller?" Grady asked.

"I don't trust anybody, but he comes close."

"He don't smell very honest," Grady said with a grin suddenly taking over his big face.

"That's the only kind you can let come that close," Slocum said back at him. Both men laughed at that.

"You know Kilrain," the rancher said, his tone serious again. "That son of a bitch has got this country right by the balls. I just know he's running the road agents and the gambling and the whores and just about everything else. Now he wants into the horses. Probably looking for a clean front for himself."

Slocum suddenly spat in the direction of a tiny lizard, splattering the animal but not drowning it. "And everybody puts up with it on account of he's the man who can keep the lid on."

"That is correct."

"I can pick up on those men tomorrow if you want, but it won't do much good. Someone was out there with an animal about to throw his left front shoe," Slocum said.

"That do us any good?"

"Might." Slocum sniffed, looked straight up at the horizon, and said, "There's a print yonder, over by your blacksmith tent there, of the same horse."

He turned to look at the rancher as it hit.

"You sure?"

"Are you paying me to make mistakes, Grady?"

Boge Grady's big shoulders seemed to quiver and he looked down at the backs of his hands as he twirled the stem of bunchgrass in his fingers.

"You got a notion who?" His pale eyes looked straight at Slocum as he spoke.

"No, but I'm going to find out."

Again he watched it hit the big rancher.

Boge Grady nodded. "Well," he said, "that's what I hired you for, ain't it."

Slocum said nothing, but he could see that he'd opened something. Then he said, "Rounding up horses sure ain't as simple as it looks, is it?"

They were standing now and Grady let out a short laugh at the remark.

"Slocum, I want you to run this roundup. I don't care where it gets to. I want them horses. I . . ." He paused, looking into the sky again. "I need them horses." Slocum watched his jaw tighten.

"That's what I figure."

"I want that big buckskin stud. That horse is worth a fortune."

"I know."

"You get him and I'll add extra to our agreement."

"Good enough."

"Main thing is, I want you to run the whole she-bang."

"I figured that is just exactly what I was doing, Mr. Grady." Slocum had kept his tone of voice absolutely level, yet there was more in it than there had been in the earlier conversation. It was time Grady knew he couldn't have it both ways.

Suddenly the rancher chuckled. "Don't meet many like your kind any more, Slocum. You mind that?"

"I mind my own business."

Boge Grady threw back his head and laughed. "You sure know how to straighten a man out, I reckon. Come on in a minute. You got a minute? I got something I want to show you."

In a moment they had left the horse corral and crossed the yard and entered the house.

"Anybody else want that big stud?" Slocum asked as they entered Grady's office.

"I'd bet my ass on Lupis Kilrain for one. Hell, any-body who's seen that animal would give his teeth and maybe even his ass for him."

Grady had stopped at his desk and taken out a new bottle. "Got this sent special from Frisco. A whole case of the stuff. It ain't no Indian River poison."

Slocum grinned, pushing his hat farther back on his head as he accepted the glass and held it while Grady poured generously. The aroma of good strong whiskey swept to their nostrils as they lifted their glasses in a toast.

"To the good old days," Boge Grady intoned. "May they never come back."

Laughing, they drank.

The rancher put down his glass, letting his breath out

hard, filling the room with the smell of whiskey. He walked to the window. "I want to tell you something."

Slocum had moved over by a wall and was squatting on his heels. Looking at him there, Grady laughed again.

"You can always tell a man of the trail. When he's in a house, by God, he's still like he's out in the mountains."

"I just like to be near the outside when I'm in," Slocum said with a friendly laugh.

"I know what you mean." And he repeated softly, as though to himself, "I know what you mean." He had slipped the palms of his hands inside his wide belt and now he stood with his legs spread, looking out at the sun settling down into the horizon.

The big window was flooded with gold and the light of the sun even reached far into the room to wash along the walls and light up a picture of a woman standing in a frame on a small table by the horsehair sofa. Slocum wondered idly who the woman was—maybe Grady's wife.

"I'll tell you something, Slocum." Grady turned to face his companion. And still he paused, as though having difficulty in ordering his thoughts, choosing his words, or maybe even in speaking at all.

Then he said, "See, you're an old-timer. Oh, I know, you're still young. A lot younger than me and my likes. But you know the old ways. I seen that. I knew that when I wrote you. I can smell those things. When old Snake Poison Billy Wish told me about you, and what else I'd heard too, I figured you were the man for me. That you were one of us. I mean, a man like you knows what it is to build yourself into, say, a top hand. To build something out of nothing maybe, or at least, damn little." He nodded as though agreeing with himself. "These here men now, the young ones, they ain't like that. They're all mush once you get past the fancy shirts. But this town, the country hereabouts, it's all going fast, Slocum. Killings, and not just killings either —robberies and rape. Rape. I dunno. Maybe Kilrain isn't running it. Maybe that's just my suspicions. But about a year ago everything started getting worse. A helluva lot worse. And he changed. Got all kind of— well, more puffed up. Not so nice as he used to be. Got bossy and like that. Spreading himself all over the place."

"The law isn't worth a fart in hell is what you're saying." Rising up from his squatting position, Slocum walked over to one of the leather-covered chairs and sat down.

"The law is Lupis Kilrain and his half-assed deputies. Slocum, if I was even ten years younger, I'd clean this country out quicker'n a man can scratch his own left ball. I'd really ream those scum out of here. I remember when this was country. Cattle country, buffalo. You see any buffalo now? Hah!" He had crossed the room to pick up his drink and, swallowing, he reached for the bottle in his very next movement, hardly breaking his rhythm, and poured for both of them.

He stood in front of his companion, breathing heavily. His face was red. "Well, enough of that. What I'm getting at is, this is my last play. I am making my stake. Don't laugh. I know I look like I've got it all. But I have been taking losses, and I cannot afford to take any more." He raised his head, his eyes looking up to the ceiling. "I will not take any more! This horse hunt now, and what it could lead to, a whole new setup; I need it. And I am counting on you, Slocum. I ain't aiming to lose the Double Box!" And he added, "Not to that Limey son of a bitch, by Jesus!"

Slocum had kept his eyes close on the rancher, feeling him, knowing what he was going through with each word, each gesture.

"Another?"

Slocum stood up. "That'll do me." His eyes fell to the photograph of the woman on the table. And before he could look away Grady was speaking again.

"That's Annie. That's my Annie."

Slocum brought his Stetson hat farther forward on his head so that the brim was low over his brow. He accepted the Havana cigar the rancher offered him now and with it clamped unlighted between his teeth he walked to the door of the room. He didn't need Grady to tell him that Annie was no longer around.

Outside the twilight had almost turned to night, and as he crossed the yard to go to his horse a man's figure detached itself from the hitch rack and started toward the cabin.

"Good evening, Mr. Slocum." The voice was one he had never heard before. It was soft, cultured, British. He wondered who could be calling on Boge Grady. Or —the thought flashed like lightning through him—perhaps the man lived there at the Double Box.

At the hitch rack he took the reins of his horse, swiftly checked his saddle rigging, and was about to step into the stirrup when something struck him. Groundhitching his horse, he walked over to the only other horse at the rail. He looked back at the house, seeing no sign of anyone. Then, gentling the animal, he slid his hand down along the animal's left foreleg and lifted the foot. Feeling, he found the shoe was on snug. Squatting now, he held the hoof in his lap with one hand, struck a lucifer with his thumbnail, and examined the shoe. It was new. The animal had only recently been shod.

Dropping the foot, he stood up and looked again toward the house. Who had passed him on the way to Boge Grady? He was thinking of the print he had seen out at the box canyon.

Who was in there with Bogardus Grady? An Englishman. Wasn't Sonny Clifford English? Grady had mentioned Clifford. The accent had been clearly British, crisp, arrogant, like the men from the English cattle companies Slocum ran into from time to time. It had to be Clifford. And what could he have been doing out at that box canyon with Kilrain's men shooting at a bunch of horses?

6

Boge Grady was still getting the last of his crew of horse wranglers together, so Slocum decided there was time to bring in some game. He was also interested in taking another look at the McCone wagon train, and so one morning he found himself out at the meadow looking down into the ravine at the broken wagons, and dispersed bodies of horses and men. He had heard that a burial party was being sent out by Sheriff Kilrain, and he wanted to see what he might turn up before the remains of the tragedy disappeared. He'd also established the fact, through Grady, that there had been no women or children in the party that had started out with such hopes in the fall and had ended up in such tragedy. That was at least something to be grateful for, he was thinking as he left the spotted pony and dun packhorse in the meadow and climbed down to the site of the train of wagons that was still pretty much covered with snow.

After an hour he found nothing new, only the marks of brutality on two of the bodies. There was no question about it being murder and robbery. But there was no sign of the perpetrators. Nature had wiped out any possibility of evidence: the snow, the cold, and the wolves and coyotes that had spread parts of the bodies over the landscape. At one moment he found himself thinking of the little locket he had found and which Kilrain and his deputies had taken when he'd been arrested. As he left the scene, climbing slowly back up to the meadow where he had picketed the horses, he felt again the callousness of the act. Killing a man in a fight was one thing; he had done that and seen it done more times than he cared to remember. But murder in cold blood was something quite different.

At the meadow he also took time to look around, but found nothing. It was noon as he mounted up and rode away. The hand that he had first discovered was no longer where he'd last seen it. Evidently some wild animal had removed it.

He let the spotted horse have its head now as they rode along the thin trail. He sniffed the wetness in the early afternoon air. The thaw was overdue, but a man had to take things whenever they came. Coming to a flat place, he reined the horse and let his eyes sweep slowly through the land below him. They were above the timberline and the air was thinner, colder.

As they climbed higher his pony's shoes rang on the scoured rock. He was riding light, for all his big size, his knees taking up the spring, making it easy on the horse. To sit in the saddle like a bag of sand all day long was to kill any mount. He rarely used the reins, working the animal mostly with his knees. It pained him to see a man rein in his horse with vicious jerks. A horse frothing at the mouth from a jerking bit could really get him going against its rider.

Behind him on the dun packhorse rode the butchered sheep. It had been early morning when he'd come upon the great sheep. He had awakened at his campsite not far from the wagon train and had walked through a stand of junipers to the edge of some high rocks at the edge of the steep gully that shot down several feet to the remains of the McCone wagons.

It had been the moment just when it was getting to be dawn. The sun had not yet risen, but its light was throwing into the sky from behind the great rimrocks on the other side of the valley below.

Suddenly his attention was drawn to the rocks on the other side of the chasm. They were jagged, some of them peaks, and partially covered with snow. As the light strengthened into the day his eyes caught the figure almost directly opposite him. There, standing with its four feet close together on a pinnacle of rock, was a large animal with two thick circular horns. It was facing in his direction, while to its rear rose the great white shoulders of the mountains, and behind and above them, the limitless cobalt sky.

Slocum felt his breath catch throughout his body. Though he wasn't speaking, he seemed to hear himself saying, "He is standing in another world." And he found that he had raised his Sharps, ready for a perfect shot.

Then, to his astonishment he discovered himself lowering the rifle.

"That's foolish," he said to himself, and he lifted the Sharps again.

But he was too late. The great sheep had vanished.

Somehow Slocum felt good about that. Later in the morning he'd come upon another sheep, and this time he didn't let the opportunity pass. It was a young buck he had in his sights and he dropped him with a single shot. Then he'd butchered him, disemboweling him with quick, easy strokes.

Now the trail lifted to the left, and crossed over a low neck of rock. The rock was speckled over with various kinds of mosses: brown, green, red, black, orange. Old, pocked snow lay melting to his left; tiny blue bell-like flowers were growing on his right.

They crossed a great open space, the dun horse pulling back a little on the halter rope, so that Slocum had to turn and cuss him. Here the ocher soil was matted over with short new grasses, and sprinkled with white and purple and gold flowers. Above these were several patches of tiny ferns. And again the trail sloped down.

As he rode around the shoulder of a huge rock, the sky cleared and the sun struck with a flood of brilliant light. His eyes felt over the horizon, the land immediately before him and around him. For an instant he felt uneasy. But the feeling passed, and he let his eyes soften into the landscape.

This was the country, and he realized how much he had missed it. Behind him the dun nickered, and his saddle horse picked it up. Slocum gave the horse its head, and the animal immediately headed for a patch of succulent green growing out of the spongy ground. Both horses were hungry and they snapped at the grass all around them. They were really hungry.

Slocum sat his horse, smoking a quirly, reflecting on the horse hunt and the men he would be working with. For a moment his thoughts turned to Felix O'Toole, wondering what the little man was up to and whether he was discovering anything useful in town. And finally his thoughts centered on Sonny Clifford.

Was it Clifford who had passed him outside Grady's house? It had to be. The crisp, arrogant accent. He'd heard about him. Clifford had worked for the Liverpool Cattle and Land Company and some other big outfits. He was a tough bugger under all that enamel. It struck him that Clifford could well be playing both sides against the middle, playing both Kilrain and Grady. He was not the kind of man who worked *for* anyone; he worked for Sonny Clifford. Was it Clifford who had been out riding with Sandy Grady the other day? Something told him yes. Maybe that was why Clifford was seeing Boge Grady. He remembered the bleak way the rancher had spoken of Clifford at the time of their first talk.

He finished the quirly, stubbing it out on his leather chaps, pocketing the butt. The feeling of uneasiness was covering him again. He had just ridden into the trees on the far side of the open space when he knew somebody was cutting his trail.

A pity he would be hampered with the packhorse. But he kept leading the dun even so. He'd only just made that decision when he heard the choppy bark of a coyote. Two instincts hit him almost simultaneously. First, that was no coyote, but a human. But it was no Indian either. It was a white man pretending to be Indian.

He had sensed it as he was riding into the trees, along a mountain flank thick with spruce, pine, and fir. It was actually something that had warned the horses. He had felt it quivering through the spotted pony. Now he dismounted quickly and picketed the dun, hiding him in thick brush, then remounted his saddle pony. An ambush ahead? He listened, waiting for the coyote call, but it didn't repeat.

Turning his horse now, he rode him back out of the trees and into the open, then rode back down the trail at a fast gallop. After about three hundred yards he swerved sharply. Leaving the game trail, he headed up toward a promontory where he hoped to be able to see over a wide open area.

But he was disappointed. He could only see a few hundred feet. He listened; he smelled the air. The spotted pony lifted his ears toward the direction from which they had just come. What had warned him? In the country there were so many things that gave signals: the ground squirrel, the coyote, wolf, wren, chipmunk, jay; the world of nature was filled with this great telling, and a man had only to listen. Something had told him that there was an enemy about, maybe following him, maybe lying ahead in ambush.

He was riding a fast horse, and since he was unhampered by the packhorse, he decided on an old trick. Going at top speed, he came down from the high place and took another trail, looking for a place with ledges, preferably high up. It was a stratagem used by the mountain lion and he had watched that animal in action some years ago, waiting on a high ledge while its prey —it had been a deer—came to its customary watering hole. The cat had waited with limitless patience. Then at the precise moment it had leaped onto the back of the deer, sinking its great claws into the animal's shoulders and at the same instant reaching for the deer's throat with its long, powerful teeth.

Slocum was trying to find a vantage point where he would leave the trail, drop from his horse, and swiftly meet his enemy. For two miles he forced the spotted pony to go as fast as it could. Then he saw the place he wanted. The trail ran around a hill. Just past the point was a stand of trees. Rushing off the trail and going a good hundred yards into the timber, he dropped down. Leaving the lathered animal to recover its wind, Slocum ran forward and stood behind a big tree.

And there they were: two white men riding briskly down the trail, coming right toward him. He could easily have killed them.

Instead, he hastened back through the trees and up the hill, finding the bluff above the trail from where he could look right down on the two riders. They were well armed; gunslingers, he figured, and there was no question in his mind that they were after him.

"Hold it!" The two words hit them like bullets. "Pull up!" To make sure they understood, he snapped a shot from his Winchester close to the nearest rider.

They didn't hesitate, drawing rein instantly, their horses pulling back onto their haunches.

"You looking for me, are you?"

The man farthest away started to turn his head.

"Don't look up here. All you'll see is this barrel hole, and not for long."

They froze, their horses sashaying about as they tried to control them.

"Who sent you?"

"No—"

The bullet came within inches of the man who had started to say "Nobody."

They looked at each other, fast.

"We wasn't doing anything, Slocum. We was just watching you."

"I asked you a question." Slocum's words were the

last he was going to spend. The men knew that; he could tell.

One of the pair did turn his head then. He couldn't help it; he was shaking. "It was Grady ordered it."

"Grady, huh?" Slocum was able to cover his surprise by sounding matter-of-fact. Then he realized something. "Did Grady tell you himself, in person? You say he ordered it."

"No," said the other rider, speaking swiftly now. "It was Clifford. He said it was Grady's order."

"That sounds better." He let a beat pass. "Now get this. You're lucky I don't kill you both. If I find you cutting my trail again, you're dead. And you tell Clifford one thing. If he wants to know what I'm up to, then he can come and ask me. You understand? Do you hear me?"

Both nodded vigorously, grunting assent.

"Now then, get out of here!"

He waited till they were out of sight, dusting fast down the trail. Then he moved quickly back to the spotted pony, and rode back to where he had hidden the dun.

It seemed about time he had a little talk with Mr. Sonny Clifford; though maybe first he should speak with Boge Grady. Yet the two didn't look like Grady men.

Maybe Sheriff Lupis Kilrain was the man to consider. And then, too, Clifford was obviously working both sides, and maybe those two who'd been following him were more with Clifford than with either Grady or Kilrain.

The whole situation was damn slippery. Finally he decided to do nothing; and he remembered the story Chief Many Hands had told years ago about the Indian warrior who had trailed a wounded grizzly for several days, but was still cautious of coming too close, and so he remained watching downwind from the great animal who, as his pain deepened, became more and more vicious. The chief's small grandson had been there in the lodge when Slocum had been smoking with Many Hands, and finally the boy had eagerly asked, "What did Running Deer do, Grandfather?"

The old chief had taken a good moment before answering his grandson. He sucked on his short clay pipe, and Slocum could see he was watching his grandson's impatience to know what finally happened.

"Do," he said finally. "What did Running Deer do, you say. He remained watching the bear."

"But what else, Grandfather?"

Again a long pause. The chief was looking carefully at his grandson, the clay pipe guttering in the quiet of the lodge. "Running Deer watched the bear," he said finally. And Slocum could see—as could the boy—that there was no place for anything more than that.

He knew he was taking a chance riding into town, but he knew too that the sheriff would be playing a cool hand, and likely wouldn't want to push things to a showdown. The law hadn't a thing to hold him on. On the other hand, if Kilrain had sent those two guns to cut his trail it meant that the sheriff was worried. Or had it really been Clifford? Clifford working for Kilrain, or Clifford working for himself? That was more likely. In any event, Slocum felt now was a good time to see what was going on in town.

The first thing he found out when he walked into the Antelope was that a man named Hard Winter Henley had been shot in the chest late the night before in an altercation over cards; but while Hard Winter had been

pronounced dead not once but twice by Doc Roybee, he
was still with the citizens of Red Butte, many of whom
were now crowded into the Antelope, where a lively
betting was in progress.

Hard Winter's opponent was deader than he was,
however, and his corpse had been carried to the under-
taker. Hard Winter himself was in a bad way.

"I still don't believe he's gonna make it," Slocum
heard a man say as he walked into the scene where Hard
Winter was lying flat on his back on a pool table.

"I got another fifty says he will," a voice said near
Slocum.

"Gotcha," said the first speaker.

"There is room for more bets," the bartender intoned
from the sober side of the bar. He was a tall, gloomy
man with a voice that rolled down his thin chest.

Slocum suddenly saw Felix O'Toole beckoning him
from the door of the saloon. The little man was very
excited as he retreated back into the street.

"Slocum, I been doing what you told me."

"Watching? What did you find out?"

"I seen that person," the little counterfeiter said, his
voice almost sobbing.

Slocum looked at him. Indeed, Felix did look distressed. He was pale, his hand was shaking as his
fingers touched the corner of his mouth.

"Sweetheart?" Slocum asked. "That who you're talking about?"

O'Toole was beyond words. His derby hat, still loose
on his little round head, simply nodded. A rush of
breath, laced with the odor of stale tobacco and trail
whiskey, swept toward Slocum. "I saw her entering the
sheriff's office."

"He arrested her? Or she's working for the law? Which?"

"Neither!" Suddenly Felix stood firm as a Napoleon in the dirt street. "That poor, wretched woman was forced to—to do carnal things with that filthy old cadaver." Tears stood in his eyes. "It is horrible, Slocum. The man should be horsewhipped! Forcing a young girl to have carnal relations with him under the threat of being put in jail or ordered out of town! Can you believe that?"

"I sure can." Privately he was thinking that neither Kilrain nor anybody else had to force Sweetheart into any such position. The lady appeared to him to be only too glad to oblige any time and any place. But now, seeing how truly distressed his friend was, he began to realize the awful truth.

"Felix, you are soft on that lady, I will bet my bottom dollar."

"That is correct, Slocum. I have been dancing attendance on Miss Moon, as the saying goes."

"You mean you've been screwing her."

Felix O'Toole's little eyes squeezed shut. He managed a nod.

"How do you happen to know all this, Felix? Were you following her, or something like that?"

"No, I didn't attempt anything so bold and obvious. After all, she could easily have recognized me and what I was up to. No—I was watching the sheriff's office. I saw her go in. And an hour later I saw her come out."

"You figure they were screwing."

"I didn't think they were playing jacks or better in there," the little man said with sudden harshness.

Slocum smiled. "It's still daylight. Think I'll mosey

on over to maybe see Sheriff Kilrain. I'm getting a notion he had a couple of his boys watching me, by golly. Though they claimed they were working for somebody else."

"Can I come with you?"

"Shouldn't you be off somewhere making money?"

"Slocum, I have a thousand dollars in gold eagles, newly minted. They are beautiful!"

"Sounds great," Slocum said as he started down the street with the little counterfeiter almost running to keep up.

"Want to buy some?"

"No, but I'll give you some free advice. Be careful who you talk to. Me—it's okay. Understand? But your voice carries. And you can get your ass in a real tight place before you know it. Now get going. I want to find out what Kilrain's up to."

The sheriff's office was at the far edge of town, handy to the Gold Coast. Now, as Slocum approached the building, he heard the sound of gunfire coming from behind the log jailhouse. Slocum didn't waste time looking at the little cabin, however, as he came around the office and headed toward the firing.

The sheriff of Red Butte was facing a fence that had apparently been constructed for its specific purpose, which was to hold a number and variety of pistol targets on a long shelf that was attached to it. These consisted of bottles, tin cans, boxes, stones, pieces of wood and metal, a couple of mirrors, and assorted playing cards. There were also a number of bottles hanging from the bottom of the shelf by strings.

Slocum saw immediately that Kilrain was wearing a double shooting rig, and that the left-hand holster was new, as he had noted already at the time of his arrest in the Antelope.

The sheriff was facing his targets now, not aware of his visitor. Suddenly he struck with his right hand, drew, and fired, and one of the bottles smashed. He fired again, and a second bottle exploded into smithereens. Then he shot a hole right through the center of an ace of spades. But Slocum noted his draw was slow. Then he knew why Kilrain was wearing a new left-handed rig. Obviously he had hurt his right arm or hand, and so was working with his left.

Holstering his gun, Kilrain—still without noticing Slocum's presence—took another stance, and now struck with his left hand, but he was slow. He hit nothing. He tried again and still missed. Slocum watched the hardening of the sheriff's back as he holstered the gun. Now with his right he shot three bottles and two tin cans, to be more limber.

His arm was brisk as he spun the handgun back into its holster while his left hand felt the cartridges at his belt.

"Pretty fair shooting there, Sheriff."

Kilrain spun on his heel. "How the hell did you get back here?"

"On my two feet," Slocum said pleasantly.

"Well, your two feet can either get the hell out or in—in that there log house."

"I ran into a couple of riders today out by Lincoln Ford."

"What's that to do with me?" Lupis Kilrain stood hard as a fence post, staring at Slocum. He wasn't giving an inch.

Nor was John Slocum giving anything. "It's got this

to do with you: They could have been your men, the ones you sent to the Chicago House with that cute little doll with the big nipples." And as he said those words, his hand was close to his belt. Why not? he was thinking; why the hell not? Why not flush the son of a bitch?

He watched the dark red pour into Lupis Kilrain's face. The eyes that had been laughing were now looking at him like a pair of poisoned arrows.

"I dunno what the hell you're talking about, Slocum. Now get out or I'll throw you in jail."

"On what charge?"

"I'll find whatever one I need, mister."

"I came here to tell you one thing: You keep those clowns away from me—if they were yours. If they weren't sent by you, then . . ." He paused to watch it getting into Kilrain. "Then I reckon Sonny Clifford sent them for you." He added, "Or maybe for himself."

Turning, without another word, he walked back around the log building and out into the street.

Slocum kept walking. He walked almost the whole length of the town, down to the hitching rack outside the Come-In Eatery. In a few moments he was riding out to Bogardus Grady's Double Box, and, he hoped, a good supper with some of that mountain sheep he'd shot.

"I want you to tell me what Sonny Clifford's got to do with this horse hunt," Slocum said to Grady the minute they were alone after dinner.

They had eaten some of the sheep, and it had been an enjoyable meal, especially for Slocum, with Sandy Grady joining them. She was charming, and in the light of her good looks, not to mention the sensuous movements of her body and the look she gave him now and again, he found it hard to keep his mind on business. So he'd decided the moment he and Grady were alone that he'd have it out with the rancher.

Grady was lighting a cigar, and now he offered one to Slocum.

"A good cigar helps a man think," he said.

"A good cigar is a good smoke," Slocum rejoined, trying not to let the confrontation get too heavy, yet keeping his firmness.

The rancher sat down in the big leather armchair near his rolltop desk, and Slocum sat across from him on a straight-backed chair with a cowhide seat.

"I'll tell you," Grady said. "Been meaning to. Clifford is a man I hired for protection of my stock. I run a few head up by the Hoodoo River; got a line camp on Crazy Dog Creek. About a thousand head."

"A few, huh." Slocum drew on his cigar, enjoying it.

"Not like the old days, Slocum. But I hired Clifford to keep an eye, not only on any owlhooting going on, but also on Kilrain."

"Do you trust Clifford?"

There was no hesitation in Grady's reply. "I do not." He hunched forward, his elbows on his knees. "Fact, Slocum, I hate the son of a bitch and came damn close just now to letting him know it."

"Your daughter?"

"You're sharp, Slocum."

Slocum didn't mention that he had seen Clifford and Sandy arguing out on the trail only recently. Instead he said, "What can you do about it?"

"Nothing. If she likes the son of a bitch, nothing. And if she doesn't, then she's good enough to handle it herself." He drew on his cigar, blowing smoke toward the ceiling. "As you have seen, my daughter is a willful type of person."

"A chip off the old block," Slocum said.

"I'm glad we had our talk, Slocum. Now tell me, when will you be ready to start?"

"I've been waiting on you. You said you were hiring more men."

"Hired the last this afternoon."

"Good enough." Slocum stood up. "I reckon we can start pretty directly then." With a nod at his host, he turned toward the door. "I'll get some air, then turn in."

In his cabin, Slocum sat down on the edge of his bunk and started to pull off his boots. Then he stopped, holding one boot in mid-air.

He was thinking of Lupis Kilrain learning how to shoot with his left hand as well as his right. The man was thorough; a good thing to know about him. And it didn't look long before he'd be an ace with both hands.

Meanwhile, at the Broken Dollar Saloon, Felix O'Toole was watching the love of his life dancing with a big miner. The band sawed, honked, and tinkled through a brisk rendition of "Chicken in the Breadtray," and when the music stopped the big miner didn't. He was a huge man with a heavy beard and thick hands and he kept right on dancing with Sweetheart Moon, driving his leg between hers and, as far as the horrified Felix could tell, his penis as well.

Suddenly the crowd started hooting at the couple, who were now alone on the dance floor. They roared, they shook with laughter as the big miner wiggled and drove Sweetheart Moon all over the floor, all but falling on top of her a couple of times, but regaining his balance at the last moment, to the shrieking delight of the onlookers.

"By God, she's gettin' me! She's gettin' me!" bellowed the giant, his face flushed, his hands squeezing his partner's buttocks. Finally he reached up and ripped her silk dress right down the front. "By God, I'm gettin' it!"

It was at this moment that Felix O'Toole stepped out onto the floor with the derringer in his hand and shot the enraptured miner in the back of his head. Either his aim was poor or the miner's head was extra hard, but the result was minimal. The man staggered, felt the back of his head, and, turning, his eyes fell on Felix, who was still holding the derringer.

He was about to take a step forward when a hard voice snapped into the scene and everyone in the room froze.

"Throw up your hands, both of you! You're both under arrest!"

It was Sheriff Lupis Kilrain, his Colt pointing right at the two men, and there was no arguing his command. Felix dropped the derringer, and the infuriated miner raised his great arms slowly.

"I'm gonna choke that little bastard," he said.

Sweetheart Moon had hurried through the crowd, clutching her torn dress over her bouncing breasts, to the raucous enjoyment of the onlookers.

"You'll come on down to the jail," Kilrain said, his thin face pasty white, while his eyes stared at his prisoners like laughing ice.

Clyde Dancey met the trio outside the Broken Dollar. He had been guarding the door. The big miner was more than somewhat drunk, and by now he was even amiable.

"You be a helluva pistol shot, Shorty," he said with his enormous grin, almost hugging the breath out of the thwarted O'Toole. "By Gar, that is some sweet piece of stuff, that gal! By God, she was really putting it out there, standin' up on the floor!"

"Shut your mouth!" snapped Lupis Kilrain, jamming the big Colt into the miner's ribs, to his prisoner's laughing astonishment. "Yer funnin' me, Sheriff. Me an' Shorty here now, we want somethin' to eat. And drink! You get yer helper man there, Dancey, is it? Shit, Dancey, I ain't seen you this good while; well, Sheriff, I am sayin' get Dancey here to rustle us some grub. And somethin' to wash 'er down with! I want you to know I bin *laid!*"

They had reached the sheriff's office and Kilrain told them to step inside and empty their pockets on his desk.

"I'm arresting you both for disturbing the peace," he said. "Dancey, you take Herman here out back to the jailhouse. I want to talk with O'Toole."

When the two had left, Kilrain holstered his gun. "Now then, what about our deal, O'Toole? I have been expecting you to come up with some money. Where the hell is it? And, what's more, I don't think it can be very healthy for you hanging around that brown-headed bitch over at the Broken Dollar."

Lupis Kilrain felt a lively twinge of pleasure at calling Sweetheart Moon, the love of *his* life, a brown-headed bitch.

Felix O'Toole, confronted by his rival—or, as he swiftly noted to himself, *one* of his rivals, at any rate— paled. He felt something turn in his stomach. But he had not been duping the law, the U.S. Mint, and his fellow man without learning a thing or two. With consummate speed he dropped Sweetheart Moon and all thoughts of revenge from his mind and turned his total attention to the business of money and physical survival.

"Why, of course I have been working on it, Sheriff. Been working out a better mix. It's a bonanza, I can promise you that. But you didn't say how many you wanted."

"I'll start with a thousand."

"That'll cost you five thousand dollars," Felix O'Toole said. "And those ten-dollar eagles will make you a five-thousand-dollar profit."

As he finished speaking, Felix found himself staring straight into the sheriff's laughing eyes.

"Tell me, how much?"

"Five thousand." But hesitancy had invaded his voice.

"And how much do you figure your freedom from this here jail is worth?"

Swift as a snake, Felix came up with the answer. "I'd say five thousand, Sheriff."

"That is correct!" Lupis Kilrain sniffed, spat in the general direction of the choked cuspidor, only just missing Pierre, who half rose, his back arching, and then resettled himself after giving the warning.

"I tell you," Kilrain went on, "I'm going to let you escape. Got it? You escaped. I mean, if anybody asks. On account of you don't have your equipment and tools with you. See, you need to be with them, where you can best use them." His eyes were right on the other man, brimming with laughter. "Only one thing." He canted his head to one side, arch, his eyes twinkling. "You don't deliver, you cross me, I will kill you personally, slowly." He sniffed. "Might take a half-hour, maybe more, to get it done. You got it?"

Felix O'Toole's Adam's apple pumped once in his short, stubby throat. "Got it," he said.

"Now git. Next time I see you, you'll have those gold eagles all shiny and nice. And news on when Slocum's starting his hunt."

A moment after Felix O'Toole had left, Clyde Dancey walked in.

"How's that big-mouth son of a bitch?"

"Sleeping."

"Let him sleep it off and he can go in the morning. Meanwhile, follow that little runt. Don't get your eyes off him."

As his deputy went out the door, Lupis Kilrain wondered if he would be hearing from Dancey that O'Toole had been chasing after Sweetheart Moon again. With this thought he made a sour face and spat again at the loaded spittoon. Pierre, who was lying nearby with his back to the receptacle, didn't move as the tobacco and spittle plopped in. Only the fur along the back of his neck lifted.

"Fuck you," Lupis Kilrain said, and he turned down the wick in the coal-oil lamp, leaving the room in darkness. His step was swift and eager as he hurried toward —he hoped—Sweetheart Moon.

Slocum had just pulled off his second boot when the knock came. His hand slipped instantly to his holstered sixgun.

"Who are you?" His words were neither hard nor soft, but they did not invite entry.

"It's me," said the voice, "Sandy. Can I come in? I want to talk to you."

"You alone?"

"Yes."

He opened the door, still with his hand near his gun. He had been thinking of Sonny Clifford and the slippery feeling the whole situation of Grady and Kilrain gave him.

"Come in," he said, noticing instantly that she wasn't as cool and self-possessed as he'd seen her before. "What can I do for you, lady?" He slid the bolt on the door.

"I hardly think you have to bolt us in," the girl said, tossing her head a little and holding her arms straight down at her sides.

He thought she looked marvelous. She was breathing a bit heavily, as though she'd been running. Her breasts were pushing with tantalizing rigidity against her silk lemon-colored shirt.

He grinned at her as she walked to the other end of the cabin, away from his bunk, and turned to face him. "Lady, from the way you sound and the way you look, I don't figure you're interested in the whole Territory knowing you're here in my cabin."

"Call me Sandy."

"What do you want?" He put out a straight-back chair for her to sit on.

"It's a long story, but I'll try to tell it quickly and briefly." She took a breath, her bosom straining against the shirt. He could see the outlines of her nipples, and he didn't hurry to take his eyes away.

"There's a man, a man my father hired—"

"Sonny Clifford."

"You know him?" She seemed to come to suddenly, more in the actual moment than she had been as his words caught her interest.

"Not personally."

"But you know about him."

"Maybe."

She pursed her lips. She had a wide mouth, full lips, and wide-spaced brown eyes. But it was her expression that got him. She was looking at him in a way that told him she was seeing him for the first time.

She drew her lips together in a tight line, bringing out the dimples in her cheeks as she contemplated his reply. "Maybe," she said softly, and as she looked at him he was sure her eyes turned up at the outside corners.

Suddenly she sat up straight, her legs tight together and her arms outstretched with her hands pressing lightly on her knees. "This man, Sonny Clifford, has taken a liking to me. Rather a strong liking, I fear. And . . ." She looked down. "Well, I don't even know if it's right, my telling you all this, but you see, Father is indebted to him in some way or other."

Slocum nodded. "That figures." He added, "Has it anything to do with your mother?"

He felt more than saw something jump in her at his words. "How did you know that? Did Dad say anything? I never thought he would say anything to anyone."

"He said nothing."

"Then how . . ."

"It was the way he looked at her picture, in his office the other day. And the way he said her name. I knew she wasn't dead."

"She might as well be."

"But the place she's in costs money."

"Lots."

"And Clifford . . . your father told me he hired Clifford to watch his stock, there being a good deal of rustling."

"That's what he hired him for."

"And Clifford—he moved in somehow."

"Sonny Clifford wants to take over the Double Box. I don't know why. But he's been asking me all kinds of questions, things that wouldn't interest an ordinary person or acquaintance, or even friend. Like how much this and how many that, and where and when. You know the kind of thing. I've no proof actually, but I feel he wants to take over."

"The in-between inventory stuff. I do know what you mean." His eyes rested on her lips for a moment, then lifted to her eyes. "And you—you're considered part of the inventory, are you?"

She was leaning forward now, with her forearms on her thighs which, encased in putty-colored riding pants, simply were the most inviting pair of legs Slocum had seen since he didn't bother to think when. "No, Slocum. I am not, definitely *not,* part of the inventory, or the in-between."

"But you're caught. You want to help your father."

"Not by whoring." She looked down, dropping her head suddenly, staring, he assumed, at the backs of her hands, which she was holding out, her palms facing the floor. "I don't know what to do. I want you to help me."

"What makes you think I can?"

"I believe you could if you wanted to. Anyway, you're my last hope. Clifford even says he wants to marry me."

He had been looking at her hands, which she now clenched lightly into fists, and now he saw that there were tears in her eyes.

"I might think about it," he said.

He watched her bite her lower lip. He had spoken with a certain tone that he knew she wouldn't like.

"But only if I get your full cooperation."

"I will do anything you want. Just say what."

"Take your clothes off."

She didn't move. Her brown eyes seemed to widen as she looked back at him, a tear drying on one cheek. Her mouth had been partly open, but now her lips set in a straight line, and she stood up.

"Sorry," she said. "I made a mistake." She started toward the door.

"Sit down," he said in a new voice. "I'll help you."

She turned back from the door, letting her hand fall away from the latch.

"You will?" She was suddenly not the same person at all, he saw. She was softer, more open, clearer. "And you won't insist on making love to me?"

"I won't even insist on screwing you, lady. As for making love, we'll let that take care of itself."

Catching the surprise in her face, he said, "Sometimes there's a difference, you know. Now let's cut the gabble and get down to business. What do you know about Clifford and about your father's business?"

7

Algernon Fortescue Clifford-Tynes had, as the saying goes, been born to the purple. Rich, socially ensconced in the upper waters of British aristocracy, Sonny had been, and still was, a good deal more than a black sheep. He wasn't a sheep at all. Along the way to what his family saw as his maturity he had been characterized as a wolf in the baby's pram, a poisoned apple in Eden. More lately, though, not a few people had put it as their contact with Sonny Clifford deepened, that the man was quite simply a son of a bitch.

At the moment he was seated in a room in the Chicago House, enjoying one of his favorite pastimes— counting money. Golden eagles, to be exact. As he counted he felt the small bright eyes of the little man standing on the other side of the table. Felix O'Toole's sharp little eyes were pecking all over those brand new ten-dollar gold pieces.

"They're beautiful," Felix said.

"They look absolutely authentic."

"Old-world craftsmanship, sir," said Felix with pride.

"And new-world duplicity," said Sonny Clifford with a grin.

He was a tall, slender man, his height showing even while seated. An aquiline nose, lazy eyes—which, however, missed nothing—and a dimpled chin made up a face that certain women thought handsome. Others thought it weak. But none failed to notice the man. His tone, his very vibration, almost quivering with an arrogant indolence, challenged the world. He had left England in a hurry.

"That will be one thousand dollars, Mr. Clifford," Felix O'Toole said. "You've got the merchandise at half price; a tidy sum to try it out. As you requested."

"I see."

The Englishman made no move toward his pocket, but simply continued to sit in his chair on the other side of the table, which he used as a desk, regarding the man opposite him with ease.

Felix O'Toole, on the other hand, was not easy. He looked around the room to try to calm the feeling that was beginning to invade him. It was a regular hotel bedroom, but obviously now used as an office. There were books about, clothes lying on the bed, papers on the table in front of Clifford.

Felix had picked up the gossip on Clifford right after the man had approached him in the Broken Dollar the night before and said he was interested in "making money;" that is, in buying counterfeit eagles. Felix had turned out the desired quantity in record time. Meanwhile, he'd learned that Clifford was some sort of English nobility, a black sheep, and more recently a range detective for the Stockgrowers Association. At present nobody seemed to know what he was, though all treated the subject of Sonny Clifford with caution. One oldtimer had put it to Felix that "When that feller takes a look at a man sometimes, it's like he's pissin' at you right out of those eyeballs." The man had a reputation that created a ring of suspicion around him. He was forever manipulating, insinuating, using, intimidating.

Felix had listened, but he realized now he hadn't listened well enough. Everything he had heard about Sonny Clifford was true, only more.

But Felix O'Toole had never lacked courage when it came to the mark—that is, money. Standing at his full height of five feet, five inches, he said, "You can pay me now, Mr. Clifford, and I am certain that you will find full satisfaction with the product."

A humorless smile creased Clifford's smooth white face. "I think we'll put that on account, Mr. O'Toole." Before Felix could respond to the audacity of his manner, he leaned forward on the desk. Now he said, "I am in the process of arranging certain business dealings here in Red Butte and roundabout. I think I might have a use for you."

A gargling sound came up from O'Toole's throat, but the words came out. "I want my money."

"My good man, you're going to get it. But first, while we're waiting—just to make sure the product is all that you claim—we can do a little business."

"That's not the way I do business," Felix said, standing firm.

"But it is the way I do." And opening the table

drawer in front of him, he swept the gold eagles into it, and in the same rhythm brought out a derringer. "Hah! Fancy finding this here! I knew it was somewhere about. Thought I'd lost it."

Felix O'Toole felt his ears pounding and his pale, moon-shaped face had turned gray-green. He could feel the color himself, knew that he wanted to be sick.

"I want you to help me, O'Toole. I want you to tell me about this man Slocum. His comings and goings, what he's up to out at the Double Box. I presume he's working for Grady. In what capacity? Is he—he probably is—the chief horse wrangler?"

In the silence following these words, Clifford regarded the man standing across the table with amusement. "I suppose he's after that fine stallion, the buckskin. Have you seen him?"

"No." Felix could barely get the word out.

"He's a dandy. Fantastic! I'd give my soul for that horse. If I had one." He looked at Felix O'Toole with eyes that caused a shudder to run through the little counterfeiter.

"I know nothing about Slocum," Felix said finally. "And I still want my money." He was looking right at Clifford, and the derringer lying on the tabletop was within his vision.

"I know you'll be patient," Clifford said, standing up and letting the tips of his long, slim fingers touch the top of the table.

"I guess I'll have to be," Felix said, feeling brave again and stronger in himself. "I won't do business with a man like you, Clifford."

"Oh, I wouldn't be so sure. I really think you might, O'Toole." Clifford shoved his hands into the pockets of his trousers and strode around the desk to confront the shorter man. "I believe you are acquainted with a lady, a lady by the name of Moon, Sweetheart Moon? Interesting name!"

Felix wanted to reach out and touch the top of the table for support, for a reality which Clifford's words had driven completely out of him.

Clifford was smiling. "I believe in doing business all the way, Felix. All the way. Right to the grave, you might say. I want us to understand each other." His smile was quite deadly as he looked at the man standing in front of him. "I want to hear about Slocum. And, of course, Grady too, and anything else of use to me. When they will be starting their horse hunt. How many riders they'll have. The location of the hunt. As I say, it will surely be where the buckskin is. But where is that magnificent animal? I myself have seen him only once, and then not really close." He paused and, reaching to the cluttered table, found a small box, opened it, and took out a cigar. He did not offer one to Felix O'Toole.

"I shall be expecting you—let's say tomorrow, in the afternoon. Or sooner. The sooner the better!" He gave an abrupt laugh as he stepped to the door and watched his visitor closely. "I know it would be most distressing to you if anything should happen to Miss Moon." He held up a deprecating hand. "I really don't believe anything untoward will."

After the door had closed behind Felix O'Toole, Clifford walked to the center of the room and, shrugging his shoulders a little, swept his hand to the hideout under his coat.

He smiled at the gun he held in his hand. Then, crossing to the open valise lying on a sofa on the other side of the room, he drew back some clothing. Reaching in, he brought out an apparatus that any cardsharp would have recognized as a holdout, an apparatus for slipping a card into the hand without anyone in the game being the wiser. He removed his coat, put on the holdout, then put his coat back on. This particular hold-out had been rebuilt to carry not a playing card, but a small derringer pistol.

For the next couple of hours Sonny Clifford practiced bringing his derringer down into his hand inside the sleeve of his broadcloth coat.

Slocum had listened to the girl for an hour, maybe longer. She had suddenly opened up with her whole history. The years of her mother's paralysis and finally insanity, her father's bringing her up with the assistance of hired help to take care of her, for he was on the trail much of the time or hard at work around the ranch. Later, there had been boarding school in Boston, and an eastern college.

When Boge Grady was up he'd had money to burn. And money eased the wheels through the days and nights of Annie's grim presence. Finally she'd had to go to a home.

"An asylum," Sandy said. "Let me call it straight. She was crazy as a bedbug. She'd been raped and beaten when she was a young girl, and she'd never gotten over it."

"Someone in the family?" Slocum asked gently.

For a long moment the girl was silent. He watched the curve of her cheek in the light thrown by the lamp.

"Yes," she said. "Someone in the family. It doesn't matter who. Well, since it doesn't matter . . . it was her father. I don't really know if it was that that drove her crazy. It doesn't matter now. But whatever it was, it nearly drove Daddy out of his mind with worry.

He—he loved her. I can't say anything more than that. He's still in love with her."

"I know," Slocum said quietly. "That's all there is to say. He was a lucky man."

"Lucky!" Seeing the look on his face, she caught herself. "Yes—yes, I see what you mean. I hadn't thought of it like that."

"I believe your father did."

They were silent now as they sat on the floor on buffalo rugs.

"It must be late," she said after a while. "I must be going. I've kept you up late."

He was not far from her. He reached out his hand and took hers, which had been lying lightly in the long hair of the buffalo rug.

"I should go."

"Yes, you should. I'm not keeping you."

He had moved alongside her and her sweet smell was strong to him. His lips brushed the top of her hair, then her cheek. Then, lifting her hand to his lips, he kissed her fingers, then her palm.

When his hand moved over her breast she shuddered. Her breath was warm on his eyes as he inclined his mouth toward hers.

Softly they kissed while she covered his hand as it held her breast. When he began unbuttoning her shirt, her hand dropped down to the bulge in his trousers. And in a matter of seconds she had his cock out and was stroking it full length with her soft hand. He was wet all along his shaft as he pulled off the last of her clothing and brought his rigid organ between her legs. With his fingers he began playing with her, finding the silky wet slit.

She was moaning and couldn't lie still, her entire

body was trembling as his fingers explored all along the inside of her thighs and right into her.

"Give it to me," she begged. "My God, John. Give it!" She collapsed on her back now, with her thighs spread wide apart.

He pumped her smoothly, their bodies glistening together as their sweat lathered them into a higher passion. Now they moved more swiftly, not missing a beat. Then, without any warning, he pulled out. She gasped her protest as he flipped her over, brought her up onto her hands and knees, and entered her from the rear, while she sobbed with the pleasure of it.

"Come!" she begged him. "Come, come, come, come, come!" But still he refused, keeping the exquisite moment to an eternity of joy. At last he turned her over onto her back, and slowly, very slowly he began to make love to her with slow, long, gentle strokes.

Then he began to pump faster as she locked her legs around him, but as her passion reached higher and higher her legs loosened, not falling away, still holding him, but in a new kind of tension, totally surrendering to his massive, expert maleness. In this way they rode each other to the ultimate moment when they exploded in spite of themselves.

They lay in each other's arms, ecstatically exhausted and soaking wet.

"My God, John. Why did we wait so long to come to this?" Her words whispered into his ear, and they were perfectly clear to him.

"Doesn't matter why," he said. "We're here now."

She was silent for a long moment. Then her fingers began to play on his belly, up around his nipples, down his ribs to his hips, then to his loins, tracing little routes of joy as his member rose stiffly. Finally she fisted the great thing and, still stroking, bent over and took him in her mouth and down her throat, almost choking on it, but sucking long and well, her tongue tickling along the great shaft until finally he came, almost choking her so that she had to pull away to get air. But in an instant he was on top of her again, stroking right into her. Together they stroked their rhythm faster and faster until neither could bear even a split second more and so in perfect unison they exploded in passion.

This time their rest was a little longer. The third time longer still.

"Had enough?" he asked her finally.

"No. But I'd better go." She climbed on top of him as his organ rose once again, and now she sat on him and rode him, rode him beautifully, and never fell off. Not until they had come for a fourth time, which Slocum figured had to be enough for one night. After all, as he told her, there was no point in being too greedy.

It still seemed clear to Boge Grady, clear and simple. At any rate, it should be. The United States Army had sent out word that it wanted to buy cavalry stock.

"Good horse, properly saddle broke," the captain had told him down in Cheyenne. "Soldiers aren't much good at rounding up the wild ones."

"That's meat and potatoes to me and my men, Captain," Boge had said. "How many head would you want? A hundred?"

"We'll make it a contract," the captain said eagerly. "Good sound animals, ready for training in cavalry work. I'll say a hundred dollars a horse, providing I have your word on the quality of the stock."

It was just after he returned to Red Butte following an absence of two months that he contacted Slocum. It was clear that the bandits were taking over everything and that Lupis Kilrain was helpless in the face of their depredations. Indeed, by now he had begun to suspect that Kilrain might be in cahoots with the road agents. It was still only early spring and there was time to get a crew together and even wait for Slocum.

"I'm one of the last in this part of the country," he had told Slocum. "The last big outfit. It's a new way of life taking over. Not long now 'fore us old-timers will be gone, like the buffalo." There was no self-pity in his words.

"You look pretty young for an old-timer," Slocum had said jokingly.

"I'm my age, whatever that is."

"I mean, a man can tell you're the old breed, Grady. For one thing, you don't pack a gun."

The rancher had chuckled at that. "I gave that up a while back. Once I got my spread and got known. Chisum never packed a gun, far as I know." His eyes dropped to Slocum's holster.

"I live a good bit differently than you, Grady. If I ever settle down—and it ain't likely I ever will—then I'll quit packing a sidearm."

They had both chuckled over that.

Now, sitting alone in his office at the Double Box, Boge Grady found himself thinking more of the past. "I'm getting old," he told himself. "Old men live in the past." He laughed at himself then, just as there came a knock at the door. It was Dan Duncan, his foreman.

"I hear Slocum's given orders we'll be starting the hunt beginning of next week."

"Next week!" Grady stared at this information.

"That's what they're saying."

"That's what I told 'em," said Slocum, coming in

behind the foreman. "Don't you boys get yourselves in an uproar. I say, that is what I *told* them."

"You mean we're riding out—when?" said Grady.

"In about six hours. That is, about two hours before dawn." He turned to the foreman. "But, Dan, don't tell the men till the last minute. I know Kilrain is getting ready to bring his men out when we do."

"Why is he waiting for us?" asked the foreman.

"Why should they do all the work?" Slocum said. "He'll let us round up the animals, then take 'em."

"Except the son of a bitch won't!" Grady snarled.

Slocum grinned as Duncan closed the door behind him. Then he became serious. "There's Clifford," he said. "Are you going to straighten him out, or am I?"

Boge Grady had poured a whiskey, passing the thick, heavy glass to Slocum.

"You figure he's going to pull the same deal as Kilrain, let us do the work and then take over?"

"That feller isn't playing patty cake. He is after this outfit. I don't know why. I've heard the usual rumors about maybe the railroad throwing a spur out this way, I don't know. I'm sure you've heard the same."

The rancher nodded.

"It don't matter whether this one's true and that one's not. Something's going to happen. And Clifford's in on it. Or thinks he is. Any way you slice it, he wants this outfit. You agree to that?"

He canted his head toward Grady, squinting a little from under the wide brim of his Stetson hat.

"I do agree. The man's been pussyfooting around here this good while, nibbling here and there, even nibbling at my daughter. Trouble is, he's loaned me money. That's why I need those horses, to pay the son of a bitch back and be shut of him."

"I know," Slocum said. "And that's why he'll do everything he can to bust up your deal with the Army. We've got to watch out. He can get desperate. For two reasons."

"Which are?"

"One: he might be in a tight like yourself, meaning he might really need a hit like this. And two: nobody, nobody says no to this man. I know the type. They don't give in and they don't give up. They have *got* to win. No matter the cost. Clifford is in this and he has got to win in order to go on living. You get what I'm telling you, Grady?"

The rancher was nodding as Slocum wound it up. "I do now. I see it. I have met that type before. He puts his whole self on the line. Failing means death to a man like that. I've known a couple of killers like that."

"Now you know a third one," Slocum said as he downed the last of his drink.

8

Sonny Clifford had no idea that John Slocum had guessed correctly about the proposal for a rail spur, but it wouldn't have mattered. His plans were well along and he was well-informed on the progress of the plan for laying track and going ahead with all the necessary work to make a cattle shipping center out of Red Butte. The important step, however, was the acquisition of land along the rail line, and also prime property in and around Red Butte.

Of course, the minute the news got about, real estate values would boom and the speculators would appear in droves.

Clifford had it on gilt-edged authority that the line would run right alongside Bogardus Grady's ranch. That the railroad moguls had not sent anybody to make an offer to Boge Grady was due simply to the foresight and manipulative ability of Sonny Clifford. Dealing, not to mention double-dealing, was Sonny's forte. He was smart, witty, charming, and at the same time, beneath his easygoing demeanor, firm and tough as the Rock of Gibraltar.

Sonny knew how to give ground in a business deal, and he would do so willingly, but it was never ground too near to his own interests. He was not a rich man, but he had very rich tastes. He knew his weaknesses: high living, good-looking women, the best of it all. He had other accompanying weaknesses, however: a lack of patience, and the curse of being easily bored. As a result, deals now and again had fallen through due to his loss of interest at some critical point.

He had promised himself this time in dealing with the Union Pacific that he would not allow himself to be derailed, that he would see the job through to its victorious end, no matter how pedestrian the details might appear. After all, he had Lupis Kilrain to take care of the gritty end of the stick, and at the other end there was the gorgeous Sandra Grady to hold him to the righteous path and spur him to heroic effort.

All this, and more besides, was running through his mind as he met with Lupis Kilrain in his room at the Chicago House.

Clifford had pushed the bed back against the wall and had a table brought in which he used as a desk. Actually, he had no real need for a desk, but he found it useful when dealing with people like Kilrain to have the desk as part of his equipment, giving him distance and authority.

He sat now in a wooden-backed chair behind the desk, while the sheriff of Red Butte sat opposite him. A bottle and two glasses fleshed out the tableau as they discussed the plan for taking the Grady horse herd.

"I can say that it's a jolly good thing there's more than one army post out here," Clifford said, lifting his glass to look appreciatively at the amber fluid.

"You mean, you can play one against the other?"

"Something like that."

Lupis was grinning. "I thought of that, only I run into the fact that the army pays a straight price for hosses. They're all the same." He grinned, enjoying the little dart he'd stuck into Clifford.

"That may be so." Sonny nodded in apparent agreement. "Nonetheless, there is the question of quality. And one can get special . . . well, favors, certain emoluments above and beyond those outlined in the army regulations; I'm saying when you produce something special."

"Like what?" Kilrain's hard voice sounded like he had a mouthful of little stones.

"Like that big buckskin stallion I see out there with his mares."

It was Lupis Kilrain's turn to color now, and Clifford enjoyed watching his discomfiture.

"I've got my eye on that there one," Lupis said.

A thin smile touched Clifford's eyes as they narrowed just slightly, then the corners of his mouth. "Ah, yes . . ." He let the word draw out as he sighed. "A pity, that, Kilrain. I'm afraid I've already promised that stud to our prospective business associates, if I may call them by that name."

Kilrain sat up in his chair, his eyes hardening. "I told you, you can't make deals like that with the army."

"I am not talking about the army, Kilrain. I'm talking about the Union Pacific Railroad. And it was quite necessary for me to offer a certain gentleman a special inducement so that my plan would be fully supported. And it has been. That horse must—and will—be delivered safe and sound to the gentleman in question." He paused, his eyes level on Lupis Kilrain.

Tough man that he was, Lupis didn't care too much for the expression in those pale orbs that were absolutely motionless, cold, yes—dead. Lupis moved in his chair. He said nothing. His own eyes were not laughing now.

"I take your silence as a sign that you have understood me." Sonny Clifford's words were as clipped as a new deck of marked cards.

"It's a pity," Lupis said. He nodded, indicating agreement, though not actually saying it. He had his private plan in mind for the buckskin stallion, and Clifford knew he did. Both men adjusted their thinking accordingly. Actually, it wasn't really any different from the way it had been. Neither trusted the other.

"So let's get it clear," Clifford said, bringing out a whole new tone. "You'll follow the Grady bunch, keeping watch on their roundup, letting them break the animals up to a point."

"The army don't want them wholly broke, anyways," Lupis said. "They want 'em just broke enough for their own men to work 'em into army riding."

"I already know that," Clifford said icily.

Kilrain shrugged with a silly smile on his face.

"I haven't been a range detective, as well as a number of other things out here in the West, for nothing."

"Heerd you used to work for Wells, Fargo," Lupis said, deciding on a new tack. But it didn't work.

"And then when the moment is ripe—and I will let

you know exactly what to do in the way of taking care
of Mr. Slocum—I say, when you see the moment is
ripe, you take the herd. But Slocum, we'll have to see. I
may have a use for him."

"You got your balls about you, Clifford, I'll say that
for sure."

"I appreciate the colorful manner in which you
choose to describe my business acumen, Kilrain. I just
hope that none of your men find it necessary to lose
their balls during the course of our adventures with the
Grady lot." He sat forward suddenly, slapping the palm
of his hand flat on the tabletop. "I think that does it.
We'll be talking."

Lupis Kilrain realized he had been dismissed. He
rose to his feet slowly, his eyes on Clifford, who was
already going through some papers on his desk, and
paying no further attention to the sheriff of Red Butte,
who felt like a schoolboy all of a sudden. Lupis was
angry all the way to the nearest saloon, which happened
to be the Broken Dollar.

By God, he was thinking, *by God, that man would
stare the eyes out of a brass monkey.* Some range detective! Well, he supposed it was as good a title as any. But
the Limey son of a bitch had to be a helluva lot more
than a cattle cop. He supposed all the stories he'd heard
about Mr. Sonny Clifford were true. If they weren't
they could be, and that was what counted. But, by God,
that cut no ice with Lupis Kilrain. He knew one thing,
and it was this—he, Lupis Kilrain, was going to by
God get that buckskin stud horse! Man like Clifford
could cut his mouth real fancy, no question, but when it
came to the nub, what the hell was he worth? He'd
heard plenty about Clifford, about how the Limey son

of a bitch was mighty long on talk and not so fast at backing it. Thing was now to plan on how to get that big stud.

As he walked into the Broken Dollar, Sheriff Lupis Kilrain suddenly felt good again. He knew what he wanted, by God. He knew who he was and he knew what he wanted. And when his eyes lighted on Sweetheart Moon, who had just come down from upstairs, she knew it too.

Meanwhile, Sonny Clifford settled back in his chair, folded his hands together over his belt buckle, and with his head slightly back contemplated a large brown stain in the ceiling just above him.

He was engaged in one of his favorite pastimes, which was the run-through of his biography. At thirty-five, he had led what he considered a colorful and at times highly exciting life. True, he hadn't made the large sums of money to which he was surely entitled, but once, twice even, he had come close. And this time he was going to win through. The Union Pacific was big. The U.P. was opening the whole of the West and he was getting in on it. For, what the devil! After Red Butte there would be other pastures.

He was lacking in only one thing. The one thing was in fact right to hand, in the person of Sandra Grady. He was really taken with her, more than he ever had been in the past with other women. And that was saying a lot, for he'd been around; he'd had his share. But Sandy Grady topped them all.

She was a cold thing. He had almost blown up at her when they'd been out riding recently. She'd acted so innocent, as though not having the slightest idea of what he was getting at. Innocent! Like the devil! She'd known what he was after. Well, he had backed down. Apologized! The gentleman!

He'd tried to cover his gaffe quickly by lending more money to Boge, but he was getting low himself. Thank God Haynes at the U.P. had come through with something. Well, the English title was worth something after all, false though it was. It did impress certain people. Unfortunately, Sandy Grady wasn't one of them. Still, he'd done what he could with the old man who proved agreeable.

He continued to lean back in his chair. Now, with his fingers laced in back of his head, his elbows spread wide apart, he continued to gaze at the ceiling as he thought of Sandy Grady and how he could have her.

When he heard the knock at the door his heart stopped. A tentative knock. Obviously a woman. It couldn't be! He leaned forward, bringing his arms down onto the table, and stared at the door as the knock came again. Then he heard the voice calling his name.

With a bound he was up onto his feet and had opened the door.

"May I come in?"

"But of course. Of course!" He stepped back almost in a sweeping movement to draw her into the room.

"Come in, please!" He was overjoyed, victorious, or so he felt, after the spat when they had gone riding together. "I've hardly seen you," he said. "I've been so busy, and I guess you have too. Certainly, your father and I have been trying to find a way he might go further into the horse hunting business. I'd thought he might open up his activity to sell horses to more than just this particular army post."

He had brought a chair forward for her, offering her a view of the window which opened onto the main street.

"I wanted to apologize for getting so angry with you," she said, though her tone was restrained, as though she'd rehearsed her lines. "I . . . well, I'm not saying that I have changed my mind. I am definitely not interested in your offer. But I did feel afterwards that I had been a little vehement. I mean, there's no need for us to be enemies." To her own astonishment and irritation Sandy felt herself flushing.

Sonny Clifford was cool, though fuming inside. For a moment, just for a moment when he had realized it was she coming to see him, he had hoped, had even surmised that she'd changed her mind, had capitulated. Now his hopes were dashed, but he covered with a smile.

"It's quite all right. I too spoke hastily. It's just that . . . well, you have such an effect on me, Sandy. I can't help it if it takes such a passion. You are so beautiful!"

"Please . . ." She had risen to her feet and started to the door.

He managed to get around his desk quickly to be ahead of her. "Might I escort you someplace? Would you join me for lunch?"

"Thank you. Another time." And she was gone.

He stood facing the closed door. Damn her! Obviously she was trying to oil his relationship with Boge so that the money wouldn't become an issue. She must have spoken to her father, and certainly she would know about his financial difficulties. Support for his wife in the place she was staying had to be expensive. Those sorts of institutions always were. Clifford had known that early on. But the girl would know it too. And she didn't want to do anything that would interfere with the money he had loaned Boge. Damn her! Scheming bitch! Using him that way.

He was furious as he walked out of his room and still furious as he walked into the Broken Dollar Saloon. His anger had spurred his passion for Sandy Grady. Knowing himself as he did, he knew there was only one way to take care of it. Thwarted though he was by the immediate object of his desire, he would necessarily accept secondary relief. Sonny Clifford was above all a very practical man. And as he spotted Sweetheart Moon coming down the stairs from the balcony that led to the rooms above the saloon, his anger evaporated.

"How do you want it?" she asked him sweetly as he turned the key in the lock of her door.

"Standing up."

She made a face. "Couldn't we do it lying down just this once?"

He was already unbuttoning his trousers. "Maybe next time," he said. "Next time you can pick."

And Sonny had to agree that, though Sweetheart had stated a preference contrary to his, she in no way allowed the difference of opinion to hinder their very, very good time.

Slocum was hunkered down on his heels in the middle of the horse corral at Billy Creek line camp. The men stood loosely around him as he drew in the dirt with a twig. They had ridden out of the Double Box well before daylight, covered by darkness, and had stopped off at the camp for a break to blow their horses and get the plan together.

"We'll take in an arc of about twenty miles," Slocum was saying, "until somebody spots the horses; we hope the herd led by the big buck stud. Whoever raises it will build a smoke signal. Make two fires fifty yards apart, and choke 'em with green leaves. We'll all meet there and then get started on our business."

"What if we run into trouble?" a man asked.

"You mean like Kilrain's men? Make one smoke with puffs." He went on, "If we don't find horses or any loose riders, then meet back here for breakfast tomorrow, or any time tonight you can get in."

Riding along with a somewhat nervous Felix O'Toole not far away, Slocum began to see horse signs. It was still the forenoon. The area they were covering was enormous, and even though he was sure a big herd must be roaming not too far away, he also knew it could be hidden in any one of a hundred valleys that had water holes.

Shortly past noon, he drew rein and signaled Felix. They groundhitched their horses and, taking food from their saddle packs, ate hungrily under the hot sun. While their horses cropped the short buffalo grass, Slocum made a careful study of the surrounding landscape.

"I don't see any smoke," Felix said. "Do you think we will soon?"

"Might." After a moment he added, "Might not." Slocum was staring at the horizon to the east. "Looks like it," he said, and stood up.

"Smoke!" Felix almost jumped to his feet. "Is it Injuns?"

"You got a short memory," Slocum said as he unbuckled the cinch on his saddle and then tightened it. "That's two columns. Remember?"

"Horses!"

Slocum spat into the dry ground. Then, stepping into the stirrup, he swung up and over. The spotted horse took his weight lightly and whiffled.

They made it to the smoke in about an hour and a half and found other men converging there, including

Boge Grady and Dan Duncan, the first men Slocum recognized riding in.

"Who found 'em?" he asked.

"I did," said a woman's voice.

It was Sandy Grady, and Slocum managed to cover his surprise.

"I told her she couldn't come," Grady said sourly to Slocum.

"Point is, she found some horses." Slocum turned to the girl, who looked ravishing as she sat a big bay gelding. "Where?" he said.

"Beyond that butte." She pointed.

"How many?"

"I—I'm not sure. Maybe twenty or thirty."

"That's not much," her father said.

The rest of the men were standing around listening. Some still sat their horses, having just ridden up.

"What were they doing?" Slocum asked her.

"They were heading into those big rocks behind the butte."

"We can get 'em," somebody said.

Dan Duncan asked, "Was the buckskin with 'em?"

She was shaking her head. "No. He wasn't."

"Who was leading them?" Slocum asked. He was starting to feel suspicious about something.

"A black horse seemed to be the leader."

"Hell, let's go have a look-see," said the tall hand named Slim, who had accompanied Slocum the other day when they'd run into the small herd and Kilrain's men.

"Wait a minute." Slocum's voice was hard with command. His eyes were still on the girl. "You say maybe twenty, thirty head."

She looked slightly embarrassed for just a moment,

then recovered. "I didn't actually count them one by one." Now her tone was tart.

Slocum wasn't having any of that, no matter how good-looking she was. "Lady, this is no time for personal nonsense. I am asking you straight questions. This whole thing smells to me."

He saw the flush sweep into her face, and her eyes burned at him.

"What do you mean, Slocum?" Boge Grady kicked his blue roan closer. "What smells?"

Slocum pushed his hat back on his head with his thumb just lifting the brim. "We're all set to go follow after them horses."

"Sure. That's what we're out here for, ain't it?" Grady sounded impatient.

"First, we're not interested in twenty, thirty head; I want to see the quality first, anyway. And second, I've got another question. Me and Felix just rode in from those two big cutbanks yonder. We came up this way." He pointed, and let his arm sweep the direction they had taken. "Did anyone else ride in from that direction?"

"Not me," Grady said.

Slocum's glance swept through the group as he heard the mutterings of denial.

"What about you?" he asked Sandy Grady.

"I came across the creek."

"Then someone's been out here, likely still is." He jerked his thumb over his shoulder. "Somebody riding a grain-fed horse. There's droppings. I seen it coming in just now."

He watched them, letting it sink in.

"You're maybe figuring it's Kilrain?" Boge Grady said after a moment. "Setting up something?"

"Somebody's out here. Whether or not they know

we're here yet is a question. They'd sure be happy to get us all together in one of those box canyons." He let his eyes fall on the men more directly now as his spotted horse bobbed its head at deer flies. "You men mind this now. We'll scout. We want the big herd. So we'll spread out wide. I'll be on the north end; Boge, you take the south. Duncan east, and Slim, you take the west. The rest of you men fit yourselves evenly with the four."

The men were already turning their horses.

"Where do you want me?" the girl asked.

"I want you back with the chuck wagon. And, Felix, you too. You can both help Schultzer and watch the remuda too. Casey will tell you what to do." Turning his horse, he rode right up to where Casey the remuda wrangler and Schultzer the cook were sitting their horses. "Keep an eye on those two," he said, lowering his voice. "They're green. And keep your guns handy. I don't like the way things look at all."

"You think it's Kilrain, then?" Grady said, riding up.

"It could be. We'll spread out real wide and see what's about." He squinted at the sky. "There's good daylight left. Could run into something." He spat quickly over his horse's withers and, nodding to Grady, started off at a brisk canter.

Felix O'Toole considered his escape from the clutches of Sonny Clifford as God-sent. Nobody else could possibly have extricated him from such a position as he'd been maneuvered into. He was more than grateful. He even felt, for a moment or two, the inclination to pray. But since he didn't know how, the impulse passed. He felt good in any case about his escape and about the way he had handled himself. He didn't feel so good about not having told Slocum what had occurred. In the end, good sense prevailed, and it was that evening when the men had returned from their scouting that he approached Slocum.

While they drank coffee and Slocum smoked a quirly, Felix recounted the scene between himself and Sonny Clifford.

"It shows my thinking on it was right," Slocum said when the little man had finished. "And did you do any of the things he wanted? Like spying on Sweetheart Moon?"

O'Toole shook his head. "No, I didn't. I went to see her, but I didn't spy on her."

"Why didn't you tell me about it sooner? Why did you wait?"

"I dunno." Felix O'Toole shrugged. "I would have, and I have now. But for a while there, I just didn't feel good about it. That son of a bitch stealing my money like that. And smiling! That's what I was thinking about."

"And you were thinking about Moon," Slocum said. "Cut the shit, O'Toole. You have got as much sense about women as you've got about horses, for Christ's sake. When the hell are you going to grow up?"

For some reason this reprimand brought Felix back into a good humor which had been lacking ever since his encounter with Clifford. Now he said, "I have done my growing, Slocum. I ain't going to grow even an inch more." Then, grinning slyly, "Except maybe with my whanger."

"Jesus!"

"Miss Moon has already made it grow bigger than ever!"

"Think she's smart enough to get your thousand dollars from Clifford?"

"If anyone could, she could!"

"I'll just bet, and you know how she'll do it; on her back." This sally brought Felix O'Toole's face down.

"I hate to even think of things like that, Slocum. Here I was funnin' and you go and make me feel like shit."

"You make yourself feel like shit, Felix, my lad. The thing for you to do is concentrate on business. To hell with that woman. Get your mind back on how you'll get your thousand dollars from Clifford."

"I'll get it," O'Toole said darkly. "I will get it. You know something about me, Slocum, it's this. I play a role, see. And I play it easy most of the time. Till I'm crossed. Then just watch yer ass. Oh, I don't mean you," he went on quickly. "I'm talking about the likes of that bastard Clifford." He flushed all the way from his neck up to his derby hat.

"Get some sleep," Slocum told him. "You're going to need it."

He had pitched his bedroll beyond the outer circle of the campsite, and had ordered the men not to bunch up, but to sleep far apart, so that if anyone did get to them in the night they'd be better able to maneuver.

"You're really expecting trouble, aren't you?" Boge Grady had said.

"I'd rather expect than wish later I had," Slocum had replied.

Now, as he unrolled his bedding, he heard the footstep. His horse, picketed close by, nickered low. And then he smelled the girl.

They didn't waste time. In a moment they were in his bedroll with their clothes off. He made sure his sixgun was right beside him, but he wasn't holding it in his hand as he had with Sweetheart Moon.

"Oh, thank God, thank God," she murmured. "I couldn't wait. Slocum, I couldn't wait any longer. Forgive me coming."

"You can come any time you like, lady," he whispered back into her ear. "But try to come when I do. I think it's better that way." And as he spoke he slid his rigid rod deep into her while her legs parted to receive him. Together they rode easily as he found his way further and she received every inch of his throbbing joy. Now they pumped more quickly, but not with haste; really taking their time, now increasing, now slowing down, and then finally going faster and faster as she gasped and dug her fingers into his back and buttocks, while he rode her masterfully to the ultimate peak of ecstasy. They lay together in each other's arms in total peace.

Yet he was still listening. Marvelous though it had been, he hadn't let his attention go completely. And lying there with her he hoped that soon he would be able to; that soon they could be somewhere absolutely alone, where they could both let everything go absolutely.

After she left him he slept, but lightly, half of his consciousness on the alert, ready to wake on the instant. Long before dawn he was fully awake, and up, calling in the sentries, talking to Grady and Duncan about the plan for the day.

They spent the day scouting again, keeping well clear of the area where Sandy had seen the horses. The girl and Felix O'Toole again remained with the wagon carrying the men's duffel, horse-shoeing materials, and cooking equipment.

About noon Slocum began seeing more and more horse droppings, cropped grass where the mustangs had

fed, and other signs of a large herd. He had also reminded the men to look for wagon tracks, for Kilrain
could have a sizeable crew with him and would need a
wagon. But there were no wagon tracks where he was
now, up north of the area known as Horsehead. The
country was wild, totally uninhabited by humans. He
kept following the signs which led him further north and
west, deeper into the mountains.

At a watering hole he found a great many tracks. It
had to be a large herd. Was the buckskin with them? He
checked closely to see if there were any riders following
the herd. Apparently only he had found the trail left by
the mustangs.

Riding now into a flat lowland he saw the three
streams. The area was rich with grass. The sun was
slanting down to the tops of the mountains as he rode
toward where the three streams converged. The light of
the last of the day shone brilliant across the rich
meadow.

Then he saw them. The long, long sunlight suddenly
shone on the backs of the massive herd. There must
have been at least a couple of hundred mustangs there.
His heart quickened at the sight.

Then, even though he had reined his pony and both
man and horse were absolutely still and that long distance from the herd, suddenly one of the horses lifted its
head. It was the buckskin, his black mane tumbling over
his brow and down along his lion-colored neck. The
stallion had obviously sensed something.

Slocum didn't move a muscle. He hardly dared
breathe. He had placed his hand along the spotted
pony's neck so he would stay quiet, and was humming
to him, saying singsong words. He wanted nothing to
break that remarkable tableau of that sea of horses crop-

ping at the lush grass, with their leader standing in his full majesty, his head high above the backs of the other mustangs, his eyes looking everywhere, his black velvet nostrils quivering, his tawny ears up and forward as he listened to the wind, the breathing of his charges, the life of the meadow.

Slocum's breath had caught in his chest. Standing there with the golden light of the dying sun washing over him and the feeding mustangs the great buckskin looked more like a god than a mere horse.

At last he was satisfied. He dropped his head, bit at some deer flies, and Slocum turned his horse and got away without being seen.

It was of course too late for a run that day, he told himself, riding back to camp. But he knew where the buckskin would bed them down, and they would find them in the morning. By golly, that stud horse sure knew how to pick a home.

At supper he talked the situation over with Grady and some of the others. Schultzer the cook had shot five tender young jackrabbits which went fine in a dumpling stew, and he used more dumplings in a dried-apple cobbler. Slocum posted guards and everyone turned in.

In the night she came to him again, more eager than ever. Just before he dropped off to sleep Slocum told himself he couldn't have asked for more.

9

Slocum knew exactly what sort of campaign he would use to round up the mustangs. You couldn't just go into the herd and start roping. Those wild horses would sight or scent a man before he even got close to them. The method was to run them down, tire them out, or resort to the more tedious method of trapping them.

"I think we'll run 'em," he told Boge Grady. "It's quicker that way, and it's sure a helluva lot more fun."

"That sounds marvelous," said Sandy Grady, over-hearing them as she walked by. "Can I get either of you gentlemen more coffee?" she asked, realizing by the frown on Slocum's face that she'd said the wrong thing again. Both Slocum and Grady handed her their empty cups.

"I realize I said the wrong thing, Mr. Slocum, about

the horses; but may I please join the hunt? I promise not to get in the way."

Boge Grady snorted. "Notice she doesn't bother to ask her father if it's all right."

"Father, I understand that Mr. Slocum is in charge of the horse hunt, and anyway, I *am* over twenty-one!"

Slocum had trouble not smiling at the exchange. "It's all right with me, lady. Just be sure you don't get in the way, and stay back when we get up close. Those animals have a keen sense of smell."

Mocking him, she smiled wickedly with all her teeth and said, "So do I—in respect to some of those men over there." She nodded in the direction of two of the more ragged-looking members of the crew.

Slocum could only shrug at that. "I reckon nobody told them you were going to join us, lady. And anyway, it ain't Saturday."

"And do be good enough to stop calling me 'lady,' gentleman!"

They all three laughed at that as she turned and walked briskly away.

"She'd make a man quite a handful of wife," Grady said, muttering into his steaming coffee, not meeting Slocum's glance.

"Reckon," Slocum muttered.

Then Grady said, "Afraid that's what Clifford wants."

"Have you heard anything from him?"

"Not in a few days. I was wondering what he was up to."

"We might find out soon enough. Let's get to the horses."

"Sure." Grady tossed his coffee grounds at the fire

ashes. "You don't reckon it'd be more sure to trap them?"

"It'd take several days of work building corrals and trap gates around water holes. That would play right into Kilrain's hands."

"Right enough," Grady agreed, and mounted his horse.

Slocum had ordered Slim Willoughby to flush the horses. The wranglers now simply rode toward the herd, so as to start them running in a direction that Slocum had indicated. He was staying on the downwind side of the animals and was able to ride fairly close and so keep a watch on them.

There was the big buckskin, leading out! Again he felt his breath catch, and looking over at the girl who was riding near her father he saw the excitement in her face.

Slocum watched as the stallion's fine tail extended behind him and he saw how the wind caught his mane. The big horse snorted, reared up a few times and pawed the air, whinnied meaningfully, and bucked just out of good high spirits. It was all in the role of leadership. The buckskin stallion, as Slocum saw it, was an outlaw king. As he streamed off with his loyal followers, Slocum could tally them better.

"I reckon two-fifty," he called over to Boge Grady.

"By God, that's a real right number!" the rancher called back.

Slocum ordered some men to take off and keep the herd swinging down toward a red rim of land in the country below. The men now began to guide the herd into a great arc or circle, the way Slocum had mapped it out on the ground at breakfast.

"Run them until they're about to drop," he ordered. He turned to Casey, the wrangler, waving his hand at Sandy Grady to ride over to where he was. "You two, you'll have fresh horses at the points I showed on the map. You pick up the winded ones, get them water, let them eat some. And keep replacing them. If you need help, an extra hand, you holler. Don't wait on it."

The circle Slocum had mapped was roughly six miles across. That made it sixteen or so around, and the wild herd was being unwittingly guided around it. It meant climbing up some hills, over a few low cliffs, fording some streams, going through brush. But it enabled the men to handle the animals well, because they could cut across the circle or across a smaller arc and not waste a lot of time in the actual running with them.

That way the wild mustangs were given no rest all day long. Slocum was everywhere, ordering the men to keep up the pace. "Run them! Run them!" he shouted.

With fresh saddle horses every little while, the men kept up the burning pace. About halfway through the afternoon, as Slocum had planned, everyone converged on the fleeing horses and guided them into a box canyon with a narrow opening. It made a natural corral which could be closed at the low entrance by having a couple of men on guard and maybe stretching ropes. For Slocum it suited the purpose beautifully.

The horses didn't race in. Not a one of them bucked or pawed or kicked now. Not one reared or tried being frisky. They trotted or walked fast or struggled to gallop slowly. But their fine heads hung low and their coats were lathered with sweat. From sheer exhaustion the fight had been knocked out of them. Slocum wasted no time in taking advantage.

"They're done for," Grady said, riding up to where

Slocum was sitting his tired horse. "They're dead tired. And I am too. How's your roping arm?"

Slocum didn't answer. Standing in his stirrups he called to Dan Duncan, "You and me, we'll take the first shift. The rest will stand by."

He had taken his rope from his saddle and was already building a loop. He saw that Grady's foreman was following suit. Slocum had picked only one other roper beside himself, at least for the present. It had been a while since he had done much roping, other than dabbing a loop on his horse when he roped him out of a remuda. But his arm felt good.

"You going for the buckskin, Slocum?" Grady asked with a big grin.

"How'd you figure that?"

Slocum was riding his spotted pony, knowing him best, trusting him as his best mount. He rode near to the sweating, blowing animals quietly, with no noise or unnecessary gestures.

The big stallion had his head up high. Slocum straightened in his saddle. His rope sailed around his head for a few seconds, then darted out too quickly for even the stallion to see, and settled around his tawny neck.

Slocum got the big stud out of the herd with almost no commotion, although he could see the wild one was beginning to draw on his last reserves of strength. He yanked at the rope, snorted, his eyes rolled wildly, he began to bite at the air, trying to get at the thing that was holding him around the neck. Until this moment he had been free. Freedom was all he'd known. Drawing the rope, Slocum realized this, felt it, and for a racing second felt something like sadness. It was almost too fast to acknowledge, yet it had been there.

Slocum kept up a patter of soothing talk to the wild-eyed animal, and now two more men came in to take charge. They swapped ropes with Slocum, and presently everyone was working. For a start Slocum and Dan Duncan were roping the healthiest-looking horses from the herd, the rest of the men hobbling them as a beginning to their first lesson in the civilized world of man. Slocum and the men, and Sandy Grady too, kept it up for as long as they could see by the dying daylight.

Tired as he was, Slocum could have gone on longer. He loved hard work, especially with horses, but any hard work that stirred his body always brought him more resolve never to submit to a fate such as the magnificent buckskin stallion was now suffering. Life was much too sweet to ever accept captivity.

Schultzer had cooked up some good grub again, and Slocum did justice to it, as did everyone else. None of them had tasted a bite since breakfast.

Slocum ordered four guards out, patrolling a beat slowly in order to keep themselves awake. They had instructions to rub tobacco in their eyes if they felt sleep coming on and couldn't handle it. Slocum reminded them that it wasn't just the horses they were looking out for, but humans, in the form of Kilrain and his men.

Nothing happened that night. He had told Sandy to stay away and get her sleep. He would be sleeping little himself, getting up every couple of hours to check the men, the camp, the horses.

For the next ten days Slocum had the men roping, tying, training, and breaking the mustangs. They built round horse corrals, broke the horses to rope halters, sacked them with one leg tied up so they couldn't kick or run, and generally got them used to being handled. It was hard work. Miraculously, nobody got hurt in those

ten days, at least not badly. Felix O'Toole probably suf-
fered the greatest pain, but it wasn't only to his body.

The men had finally started to accept Felix in their
own way, and showed this by razzing him. The little
counterfeiter took it well, but at one point he decided to
take on the whole bunch.

There was a tough little broomtail named Poker by
the men because he was always jabbing his head against
the corral poles, and sometimes poking his head through
one of the wider spaces. Poker bucked the saddle off
four times before the men could get it cinched.

"I am going to ride that one," Felix suddenly said, to
everyone's astonishment. They saw he wasn't fooling.
"You men claim I'll never make more'n a half-assed
hand; well, I'm gonna show you!" He was very white in
the face, but everyone could see that he was deter-
mined.

"You better not try that, Felix," Slocum said. "You
could get killed. Hell, it's no shame to pass up getting
every bone in your body broke."

"Get him saddled," said Felix. He stood just outside
the round corral, his arms down at his sides, his derby
hat jammed down so far his ears were bent.

Looking at him, Slocum had the impulse to laugh,
but suddenly the group was quiet. Everyone had collected around the corral as Felix stood there by the gate,
all five-foot-five of him, and Slocum knew he wasn't
going to back down.

Slocum stepped into the corral, along with Slim and
a man named Hendry. Slim was holding Poker's nose
and Hendry held the hackamore rope. Slocum got the
cinch right up tight.

"Shorty, can you get yer foot up there?" one of the
men called out.

"Shut up," said Slocum, without looking at the

speaker. He moved toward the animal's head and grabbed his ears.

Felix was having trouble getting his short leg up into the stirrup, but finally he grabbed the saddlehorn and some of the animal's mane and jumped and pulled himself up onto the saddle. Grunting and wheezing, he got his leg across and slipped his other foot into the stirrup. Slocum had already punched new holes in the stirrup straps after measuring from Felix's hand to his armpit for the proper length.

"You ready, Felix?" Slocum wanted to stop it, but at the same time he didn't want to. "Say the word."

Suddenly a cowboy spoke from the top rail of the corral where he was sitting smoking, waiting for the show to begin. "By God, that Shorty has got his guts, I'd allow!"

Slocum took another look at the little man sitting atop Poker, who was one second away from exploding. He almost called it off then, but he didn't. He didn't because he couldn't.

"Let 'im go!" Felix O'Toole's voice cracked over the words as simultaneously the men jumped back, releasing the feisty mustang.

"Look out!" somebody yelled.

It was a wasted warning. Poker had turned into a Kansas twister, leaping, bucking, kicking, and spinning. As one of the men later put it, that rider was out of that saddle "quicker'n shit goin' through a tin horn."

Felix landed flat on his back, the breath knocked out of him. Instantly Hendry and Slim were joined by more men to haze away the bronc so he wouldn't get stomped. It was Slocum who helped Felix O'Toole to his feet.

"You are one lucky son of a bitch," he said. "You

could've got your neck broke and God knows what else!"

Felix had finally recovered his breath and his round little face, the color of paste now, slipped into a smile as a cheer went up from the onlookers.

"It was good," Slocum said to Grady afterwards. "The men been working their asses off. They needed that."

"Shorty did it!" Grady was grinning. "And you know what tickled me? He never lost his derby hat the whole time!"

It was a day later that Slocum located the Kilrain camp a couple of miles away, hidden in a rock canyon with easy access and more than one way out. He caught the feeling as he watched them through his field glasses at dusk that they had to be supremely confident. There were a lot of them, for one thing, far outnumbering the Grady force. And they were massively armed. Clearly, Kilrain had hired talent—for gunfighting if not for horse-breaking. And clearly, too, the sheriff was waiting for Grady's men to finish their work before launching the attack for the mustangs.

Slocum, with Grady's agreement, had not had the men work on every single mustang, only the best mounts. Nor were they completely saddle-broke, only to the point where the cavalry men could work on them, completing their training for army work, adjusting the horses to their own special needs.

"Looks to me like they'll be getting impatient soon now," Slocum told Grady. "Kilrain might not want to wait till we've got the work done. Fact, as you know, we're not going to complete anything."

"So you figure they might hit us pretty soon?"

"It looked to me like they'd just moved into that camp. So they'll likely locate us more sooner than later."

"Then that'll be it," the rancher replied, staring down into his coffee mug. "You say they've got near forty men."

Slocum nodded.

"Christ! More than twice what we've got."

"They were drinking a good bit," Slocum said. "That could be bad, or it could be good—for us. It depends."

Boge Grady sniffed, shifted his position as he hunkered by the small campfire opposite John Slocum. "I always figger the best way to whip any sort of enemy is to take the fight to him," he said. "Not wait for that son of a bitch to come to us. Catch them off balance, surprise the buggers."

"They've got guards out," Slocum said. "It wouldn't be easy to sneak up on them." He ran the palm of his hand over his mouth a couple of times, as though the gesture helped his thinking. "You say it would be good to carry the surprise to Kilrain, but they outnumber us with guns and with professional killers. Let's look at it straight. Most of our men are cowpokes, they ain't gunmen."

"Well," Grady said impatiently, "what the hell are we gonna do?"

"We're going to let Kilrain surprise us," Slocum said. "That's to say, he'll *think* he's surprising us."

"How the hell you gonna do that?"

"I am studying it real close, Grady, and there is no sense in you getting a burr up your ass. Shut up and listen."

The rancher suddenly broke into a big grin. "Always did say you know how to dab a rope on me, Slocum."

"We'll just keep working. Right here. Lay for him. It's a good place. We got rocks, cover, a couple of box canyons. Good cover and ways to maneuver."

"You mean we'll act innocent, like we don't know he's anywheres around. But actually we're set for him."

"See, it's us who has the advantage."

The rancher was shaking his head dolefully. "I sure wish I could believe that."

"They'll try to slip some scouts in to have a look-see and how we're doing, how much we've got broke, how long till we're going to move back to the Double Box."

"Do you think they have already?"

Slocum shook his head. "I would have spotted them. I've been expecting them. And they've just set up where they are now. It's the closest they've been to us. So they'll likely send out some scouts tomorrow or next day. I mean, they'll scout in closer than they've been doing."

"You mean to tell me you already knew they were around?" Boge Grady's jaw had fallen open as he finished speaking.

"Nothing to get excited about. I've been scouting them this good while. Ain't that what you're paying me for?"

He stood up as the rancher, reaching his feet a little more slowly, chuckled.

"So you'll scout 'em closer tomorrow and then we can figure what we'll do, eh? Good enough."

Slocum remained standing, his eyes on the other man. Suddenly Boge Grady caught something.

Slocum could see it coming. "Yeah," he said softly.

"Shit, maybe I'm really getting old," Grady said.

"But you caught it," Slocum replied.

"I have got to be quicker than that," Grady said severely, and he spat hard into the fire.

"What would you do if you were an Indian?" Slocum asked.

"Two things. First, I wouldn't wait till tomorrow morning. And, second, I'd sure thank the Almighty or whoever it is runs things around this place that I hired you, Slocum."

Slocum allowed a smile to move from his eyes down to the rest of his face. "Just a little rust," he said, "and I handed you the oil."

Slocum hadn't mentioned to Boge Grady that he had seen Sonny Clifford's big sorrel with the four white stockings. He hadn't seen Clifford, and he hadn't seen Kilrain, but he'd spotted Big Jaw Turk Nosniffer, and Dancey, and those two gunslicks he'd braced on the trail when they'd been following him.

Something in him had kept that information about Clifford to himself. He wasn't sure where it would lead if he brought it out to Grady at this point, especially with the girl at hand. And his rule was, when in doubt let things happen.

But he was busy. It was late by the time he was satisfied with the camp preparations. First he'd called all the men together to instruct them.

"I want you to fill some jugs with water. Set 'em out in plain sight around the camp area here. Make the whole place look disorderly. And lay some drunk dummies around."

The men quickly caught on and started stuffing grass into spare trousers and shirts, putting hats and shoes on some, then sprawling the dummies about as though they were men sleeping off a big spree.

The men worked rapidly, with Sandy Grady helping. Slocum saw she was in fact doing the best work. Before dawn they had finished ten dummies, resembling men lying around conspicuously, some partially in bedrolls, some against trees, some on the bare ground or with their heads lying on saddles which they used for pillows. Four of them appeared to be holding jugs of liquor. These had been taken from the grub wagon and had originally carried molasses, but they made just the stage props that Slocum wanted now.

When the job was done, the camp looked exactly like any camp after the men had been celebrating with a drunken bout.

"See, they'll know we're done with our horse breaking, so they'll figure we celebrated," Slocum explained. "Their scouts'll come pretty soon now, and when they see we've got no outriders posted and nobody's about, they'll come in closer, real suspicious."

"And they'll see everybody drunk as a skunk," chimed in Sandy Grady. The men laughed at her high spirits.

When he had finished placing his men where he wanted them, Slocum called the girl to come to where her father was.

"Sandy," Boge Grady began.

"Daddy, I know what you're going to say."

"No, you don't," Slocum snapped. "Now just be quiet and listen to your father."

The girl almost changed color at the unexpectedness and firmness of his attack. Her father's eyebrows shot up to his scalp.

"By golly, Slocum," Grady said, "you're way ahead of me there, too."

"You don't want me to stay," Sandy said, recovering her composure, and layering it with ice as she stabbed her eyes at Slocum.

"Why don't you just shut up, lady?"

"Sandy, listen," her father pleaded. "This is no time for trying to win. Just listen! I mean, God damn it, listen to the man!"

"I ought to send you back," Slocum said, "but that might cause even more trouble if one of them happened to cut your trail." He turned quickly to Grady. "Clifford's with them. He might spot her, or one of his men might."

"Then she'd better stay here," Grady said.

"That's right." Slocum nodded. "Besides, we need an extra gun. Can you use a gun?" he asked the girl.

"Yes, I can. Which one of you shall I shoot first?"

Neither of them felt she was totally joking.

"I want you with Casey. And I want O'Toole there too. I'll show you where."

The men were gathered waiting for orders and he walked toward them.

"Kilrain's men will know the horses are in the box canyon, and we'll leave them there. Then they'll see us out here, drunk and sleeping it off. It'll look like the horses are unguarded. So, as far as they'll be able to figure, we'll be easy targets. Except we won't be. We'll be spread out yonder, near the entrance to the canyon."

Suddenly he stopped, stood stock-still, listening. "I set Slim to watching their camp. That could be him coming back to tell us maybe they're moving out."

"It is Slim," someone said from the edge of the group.

In a moment the man Slocum had been expecting walked in.

"They just sent out a scout. I think it was Kilrain and Clifford, near as I could tell, who was doing the ordering."

Slocum turned back to the men. "Quick now. Get behind rocks and brush. If there isn't any brush, cut some and stick it up to look natural. Make a good loophole. And remember this—don't a one of you shoot till I shoot first. I'll be down behind those two boulders yonder." Then he added as they broke into action, raising his voice, "Remember, this will be a scout. Nobody shoot. He is to see us all drunk and go back and report!"

He turned away and his eyes fell on the girl. She was smiling at him.

In the east, steel gray was stealing into the sky, now taking on tints of pink and gold. Slocum could feel the slow movement of the dawn heavy on his tense crew. He had stationed Slim to watch for Kilrain's scout and told him to signal instantly. Slowly, slowly, the peep of dawn became the first tip of the actual sun. Then finally the sunlight actually spread down over the camp area, illuminating the drunk dummies. It was well after eight o'clock when Slocum heard the distant whistle of a bird.

"That's him," he said to Boge Grady, who was crouched near him. "That's the signal."

Still there was no sign of life. What had Slim seen? Slocum found himself beginning to wonder. The thin cowboy had been posted on a hilltop about two hundred yards, bird flight, from where Slocum was waiting. Slocum trusted him not to show even a glimpse of himself to the enemy, but he had reported the enemy and the enemy had not shown up. So it was all right, actually, for it had to be the scout, just as he'd figured. The scout had seen the campsite with its drunks lying about, and he'd returned to Kilrain to report. It wouldn't be long now.

It must have been a good hour and a half after Slim's bird call—still long before the drunks would have awakened—that he suddenly heard the bird call again.

He could feel Boge Grady's excitement only a few yards away from him. Quickly Slocum studied the ambush again. The men were strung out down to the entrance to the box canyon, half on one side and half on the other, extending about a hundred yards. This way, if Kilrain's men should run, a miss at one end could still leave room for a hit at the other. He'd cautioned the men against shooting high, a fairly common error when the rifleman is firing down a hill.

Another twenty minutes passed. Then, just when Slocum felt his men's patience must be at the breaking point, thirty-three men came around the bend of the little stream running into the canyon, riding right into rifle range.

"Christ, look at that!" Boge Grady whispered, and swiftly checked his rifle.

"Watch it!" Slocum cautioned.

The Kilrain men rode with obvious confidence, yet with rifles in their hands. And, sure enough, there was Kilrain. Next to him was Dancey, and on the other side Big Jaw. Slocum didn't recognize any of the other men until after a moment he spotted the two he'd confronted on the trail. But there was no sign of Sonny Clifford.

They rode up at a slow, easy canter, hooves drumming on the hard ground, their horses snorting in the morning air. Slocum could actually see the grin of satisfaction on Kilrain's face, and on Dancey and Big Jaw too as they came closer.

It was easy to understand. The sheriff had caught the

whole crew of them drunk. Kilrain was probably already thinking of the profits he was going to make when he got his hands on those two hundred fifty head, and especially on that prize buckskin stud, not to mention the pleasure of beating out Grady and Slocum himself.

But where was Clifford? Slocum could sense a stirring among his own men. They'd be wondering why he didn't shoot; he was letting the Kilrain men ride right by. But he wanted to get the enemy right into the canyon proper. They were now within a quarter of a mile of the horse herd at the upper end.

Slocum waited another half-minute and then called out, "You men drop your guns. You're trapped!"

His words were drowned in a crash of gunfire as Kilrain kicked his horse out of the trail and fired at the place where he thought Slocum to be. It was a desperate shot, but the man must have known he was outgamed. Yet, even so, he was sure not going to surrender just like that.

Everyone was cutting loose now on both sides. At the same time, the Kilrain men were ducking and spurring, trying to get back out of the canyon.

Suddenly Kilrain was off his horse. It was hard to tell whether he'd jumped off or had been shot. In any case, he landed with guns blazing. One of his men let out a scream of pain, and Slocum saw him fling his rifle aside. He toppled from his horse and lay on the ground, motionless. Twice Slocum saw his body jump from the impact of more bullets pumped into him.

Two more Kilrain men were unseated then. One was sprawled face up on the ground, as though spread-eagled. The other limped, managing to get behind rock cover, so that he was momentarily safe. He was safe until two of Slocum's men worked their way around behind him, and he was promptly killed.

All this while the Kilrain men were trying to beat a retreat. One horse was trying to climb an embankment which was too steep for it. His rider was down somewhere. Later Slocum regretted that he hadn't shot the animal. The horse got downhill a few yards and into a clump of bush. It looked like its reins must have snagged there, effectively hitching it.

Lupis Kilrain saw it. While rifles echoed like thunder in the canyon, the sheriff made a run for it.

"He's getting away!" someone shouted.

It seemed to Slocum that everyone was shooting at Kilrain. It all happened with the speed of any gun battle, and in this case while he was reloading his gun. He'd just broken open his handgun when he saw Boge Grady leading the running sheriff. But the bullet only kicked up gravel and dust.

Other bullets sprinkled gravel on him as he jumped, ran, and crawled down the canyon toward the horse in the brush. He just kept moving. In that instant a fear-crazed animal dashed uphill with its rider, who was shooting fast but wildly. His sudden presence on the scene served to divert several guns. Probably fifteen or twenty bullets punctured him. He died in the saddle, and was carried on up canyon into the horse herd corralled there.

The diversion of shooting at him gave Kilrain the break he needed, for he made it to the horse in the brush and in only a moment he was up and in the saddle and racing downhill. Near him another man was also running downhill on horseback, but he was so badly wounded that he fell off. He crawled to the stream and tried to bathe his wounds. Another rider was unhorsed nearby, but not hurt. He began returning the fire from the Grady men until he was cut down.

By now Lupis Kilrain was out of range. Slocum had about decided to let him go and catch up with him later. He was still wondering what had happened to Sonny Clifford. Was the Englishman back at the Kilrain camp, or had he simply left, gone back to town, not wanting to dirty his hands with actually fighting?

Slocum also knew that the chance of Kilrain riding past the men at the front of the canyon was indeed slim. But now, to his astonishment, he saw in the distance the sheriff turning his horse further along the rise of ground that led deeper into the canyon, toward the horse herd.

Of course! Kilrain undoubtedly knew the country far better than Slocum. And if he knew there was more than one way out of the canyon, surely Kilrain would know. But he was headed for the horse herd; and that was where the girl was.

Slocum saw that Grady realized it at the same time.

Running to his horse he called to the rancher, "Casey's there, and Schultzer. And she's got a gun, too." He remembered as he urged the horse into a fast canter that he had forgotten that Felix O'Toole was also there. Not that the little man would be of much use.

It was rough going on that rocky terrain, but he pushed the horse as much as he dared. Kilrain had a big start, and topping a low rise of ground at the end of the canyon Slocum saw that the sheriff had already reached the herd. He could see that Kilrain had his gun out and was firing, bearing down on three figures who were at the corral gate guarding the Grady mustangs. He was sure one of them was the girl.

The ground was soft now and he laid into his mount with the reins like whips cutting him to further effort. The crazy son of a bitch, he was thinking; Kilrain could shoot the girl! Why the hell hadn't they kept under cover like he'd told them to? Guiding the horse with his knees now, he lifted the Winchester and tried sighting. The distance was still great and shooting from a galloping horse wasn't exactly target practice.

He had just figured his range, had taken a chance on sighting, and was about to pull the trigger when a sudden rifle shot cracked into the canyon. He saw Kilrain tumble from his saddle. Now as he pounded in and dropped from his lathered horse he found himself confronted with Sandy Grady, Schultzer, Casey, and Felix O'Toole. It was O'Toole who was holding the smoking rifle.

Looking down at the dead sheriff as Boge Grady came galloping to a stop behind him, Slocum said, "Well, Mr. O'Toole, I reckon you won't have to go to making money for the sheriff after all."

"Holy Mother of God!" Bogardus Grady's jaw had fallen open as he stared in awe at Felix O'Toole.

"The deity had nothing to do with it," Felix said, standing at his full height, and looking taller, Slocum thought. "*I* did it. I shot the bugger. He thought he could euchre me out of my business. But, worse than that, he tried to get my girl friend! He made *some* mistake!"

Grady had walked over to his daughter and put his arm around her. She was smiling weakly, overcome with relief.

"Saved in the nick of time."

Slocum took out a quirly and was getting ready to light it when Grady handed him a Havana.

Slocum nodded, accepting it.

"Got another of those, have you?" Felix O'Toole asked.

"Sure do, Shor— Felix!"

Felix's smile looked like it was going to blow his happy moon face apart.

Slocum was watching the girl. He could see that she was shaken, and he was glad.

"What are you looking so pleased about?" she asked suddenly.

"Just feeling good."

"Well, we're all glad it's over," Grady said.

"Excepting it isn't over," Slocum said.

They all turned to look at him as in the near distance the Grady horsemen came cantering in.

"What do you mean?" Boge Grady asked.

"There is still Sonny Clifford," Slocum said. He looked directly at Felix O'Toole. "For one thing, he wanted you to work for him too. But I don't want you to go getting any more funny ideas. I will be handling Mr. Clifford. You understand me?"

Felix O'Toole's derby hat bobbed twice as he nodded. "I understand you, Slocum. I squared accounts with *him*." He nodded to the body of the former sheriff of Red Butte, Mile City, and environs.

Slocum gathered the reins of his horse, who by now had regained his breathing, though he was still pretty much lathered. "The men will clean up. I'll be riding into town. I reckon you'll be riding with your daughter," he said to Grady.

"I reckon," the girl said, ruefully imitating him.

Slocum wasn't in the mood. He stepped into the saddle stirrup and mounted his horse. It was a good horse, he decided, a tough little dappled gray gelding. But he was still tired, and no good for what lay ahead. And besides, Slocum wanted his spotted pony.

It didn't take him long to rope him out of the remuda

and throw a saddle and bridle on him. He had just mounted up when he saw the girl walking over to him.

"Thank you," she said.

"What for?"

"For helping my dad."

Suddenly his sour mood vanished. He smiled at her. "Anybody with a daughter that good-looking has to be helped." Touching the brim of his Stetson hat with his forefinger, he clicked the spotted horse into a walk.

"We can be thankful it's over," she called after him.

10

Except Slocum was right; it wasn't over. There was still
Sonny Clifford. And there was Dancey and Turk Nosniffer, otherwise known as Big Jaw. Plus, who knew
how many gunmen had escaped the box canyon! Slocum hadn't gone back to count the bodies, but he knew
that there was still a sizeable cadre of gunslingers remaining. And with Clifford running the brains and Dancey and Big Jaw the guns the trouble was nowhere near
over. In fact, it could be worse, for Clifford wouldn't
have the restraint that Lupis Kilrain might have offered.
A restraint brought not out of any concern for justice or
honest behavior, but from the sheriff's own limitations.
While Sonny Clifford certainly had his limitations, the
problem was he would never have recognized any. That
was how Slocum saw it; and that was what he was so
concerned with. No, it wasn't over, by a long shot!

There was only one way he could see to stop Sonny

Clifford from taking over the Double Box, and likely wiping out both Gradys, or at least Boge. And it brought a grim ironic smile to his face as he rode fast toward Red Butte. It was always the same way. It always boiled down to the same answer. It always came down to gun against gun.

What was important now was that he call the shots. He had to work it so the battle would be on his ground, his terms, in his time and place. But he knew Sonny Clifford's weaknesses—his curiosity and his vanity. Both could lead to a lack of attention at a critical moment. In short, Clifford was lacking in discipline. The thing was, though, that with Dancey and Big Jaw siding him, maybe he wouldn't miss it.

Slocum knew that the best way to handle it now would be to confront each of the three of them separately, or at least not all three together. He could even handle two. The question was how. If Clifford was as smart as he took him to be, he wouldn't be letting his two gunmen out of his sight.

At the same time, Slocum was sure Clifford would be pointing toward a confrontation with him. Like himself, he would see that the only way to settle things would be with guns. The obvious first step then would be to try for a bushwhacking.

It was close to nightfall when he came within sight of the town and drew rein by a creek to let his horse water and rest.

They would be watching the hotel, the saloons. They could even have outriders on the trail leading in. He knew they hadn't cut his trail as yet; he'd been especially careful, stopping every now and again to listen, to check his back trail.

On the other hand, they could try for Boge out at the

Double Box. But Boge had men around him, and he'd warned him to be extra careful. The rancher had promised him he would, and that he'd be watching Sandy closely. Slocum knew it was himself Clifford would be after. He would definitely see him as the key. Without him in the picture, Clifford could handle Boge Grady simply by overwhelming him.

The sun was setting quickly now, or so it seemed to Slocum, knowing it was because it was so close to the horizon. He had always marveled at the sunrise and sunset, how his sense of time and space changed the moment the sun was free of the proximity of the land. High in the vast sky it seemed not to move at all, while at the horizon one could actually notice movement.

There was just a tip of the red circle showing above the distant strip of the earth when he heard the dry wood snap. A mild sound, it could have been anything. But Slocum had dropped down, drawing his Colt in the same action. As the sun went down.

He waited. Only the breathing of the land. It could have been an animal, only he knew it wasn't. But how could anyone have slipped up on him? He knew the answer to that before the words even registered in his mind. Whoever it was had been there already. Somebody could easily have seen him riding across the open stretch to the creek, someone who might well have known he would be coming this way, for it was just beyond the creek that he could branch off either to the Double Box or toward Red Butte. It was an ideal spot.

Quickly, he went through the maneuver. Clifford must have seen how the battle was going and had drawn off, probably taking some men with him, and had set up an ambush that he could use if necessary, or not, as the situation might call for.

Undoubtedly whoever it was—and it could be a few —was waiting for darkness, which was coming fast. Swiftly, Slocum untied his blanket roll from his pony's saddle skirt and began preparing camp. He moved the spotted pony to a more hidden place near some willows, and checked his rigging, leaving him ground-hitched so that he could make a fast break for it if necessary.

Then, locating a covered spot near some cottonwoods, he spread his bedding. It was still light enough to see what he was doing, even with the sun gone, and he realized of course that he was visible. He kept well under cover, but not so anyone watching him would see that he knew he wasn't alone. He placed his bedding well into the trees, and near a deadfall. Then, working quickly and soundlessly, he stuffed the blanket to make it look as though someone was lying there. With a second blanket he cut some strips and wrapped his feet, tying his new footgear with strips of whang leather that he always carried with him. He worked swiftly but carefully and in total silence. When he was ready he stood up. He could move much more quietly now. It was a trick he had learned from the Indians.

Now he slipped through the trees, moving slowly, not even allowing his breathing to make a sound. He had already checked his Colt and the Winchester. He didn't move far away, but kept in close contact with his dummy. Whoever was out there would move in for the attack sooner or later. The only difficult question was how many there were.

It was cooler now, but not unpleasant. The smells were richer coming from the land, and the various sounds in the earth and trees were more keen. Slocum waited.

Then he heard it again, the swish of a green branch. The crack of a rifle firing at close range broke through his camp and he saw the dummy plunge under the impact of the bullet. But Slocum had also seen the flash where the bushwhacker was firing from. Without an instant's hesitation he raised his Winchester and fired. He heard a sound like a sob and a grunt together, and something fell in the underbrush to his left. Then there was silence.

He waited. He waited a long time until he was sure. Then, moving silently, he worked his way toward the man who had tried to kill him.

The body was lying face down. He'd been shot through the chest and killed instantly. Nearby his horse waited patiently. When he turned the body over and looked at the man's face under the light of a lucifer he struck for the purpose, he saw it was someone he didn't know. It could have been any one of Clifford's or Kilrain's men. One of the hired guns, who had just lost his job.

Slocum rose to his feet. There could be others along the way. But there was no sense remaining here. He rolled up his bedding, removed the strips of blanket from his feet, and within five minutes he had mounted his horse and was on his way.

That still left Clifford and Dancey and Big Jaw, not to mention how many other unknowns. But those three were the principal factors. Yet he was pretty sure if Clifford hadn't been in the picture the other two would have faded into the background. He couldn't see Clyde Dancey or Big Jaw Turk Nosniffer as whipsawing anything like some land grants or even a big horse wrangle. They were the axe and saw type, the executioners who carried out orders from a higher place. Perfect hands for a man like Lupis Kilrain and for Sonny Clifford. But not leaders.

It was about halfway through the next forenoon that he knew someone had cut his trail, so as soon as he found a likely place to turn off the trail, he did so, cutting back in a wide circle to come up on the lone horseman from his rear. The lone horseman turned out to be none other than Felix O'Toole, who was indeed riding hell-for-leather on an old crowbait bay who looked like it was on its last ride.

Felix was overwhelmed when Slocum caught up with him, overwhelmed with relief and pleasure.

"Slocum!" He was almost frothing at the mouth with excitement as he reined in the old nag who came to a limping walk, while its rider was almost bounced out of his saddle. "Slocum!" O'Toole was sweating, gasping for air, trying to stay in the saddle, and grimacing as he came down viciously on his crotch and scraped more skin off the inside of his thighs. "Slocum! I been trying to catch up with you! One of the men that got caught talked to Grady and said as how Sonny Clifford was sending somebody to drygulch you. I got here quick as I could to warn you!"

"I do appreciate it, Felix."

They had both drawn rein now and while their horses dropped their heads to crop at some of the buffalo grass that was just greening around them, they sat easy in their saddles—at least Slocum did—and under the hot blue sky took their ease for a minute. In no way did Slocum lower his guard.

"What will you do about that, Slocum?" his companion asked. "Man could be laying around about here even!"

"He is actually laying a good piece back the way you came," Slocum said easily. "Course, there might be others. A man never knows."

O'Toole's eyebrows shot to his hairline. "What do you mean?" he said, still catching his breath. "You're in danger, friend. And I am here to help you."

Slocum couldn't restrain the smile that sprang to his face, and the good feeling he had for the little counterfeiter swept through him. He had a sudden flash of Felix O'Toole astride Poker.

"I value your concern, Felix. And maybe the both of us can take out the rest of that gang. But that feller back yonder is as dead as he can ever get." He spat suddenly over his horse's withers. "So we'll just have to see what's coming up." He lifted his reins. "I am heading for Red Butte."

"By golly," Felix O'Toole said, his round face shiny as a fresh apple. "Me too."

They had ridden only a few minutes when Slocum suddenly drew rein. O'Toole followed suit.

"What's up, Slocum? You see something?"

"You want to help me, Felix?"

"That is what I been tellin' you," O'Toole said eagerly. He added, "I mean, within reason. I have got my limits like the next man."

"That trail there leads to Grady's outfit. I want you to ride there and stay till Boge and the girl get back, unless maybe they are there already."

"Why can't I go with you?" Felix asked, his face falling.

"On account of I want you to go there." He waited a beat and when the other man said nothing, he went on, "It could be Clifford might make a hit there. I know Grady's got his foreman and some good hands with him. But it would be good if you were there to take a hand if needed, and to keep an eye out for Sandra."

"Shit," said the little man, pouting a little. "But I'll do what you say. On the other hand, who is going to take care of my girl friend in town if the lead starts flying?"

Slocum sniffed at that. Then, squinting at his companion, he said, "I don't reckon any more than you do, Felix, that Sweetheart needs anybody to have to take care of her."

And with Felix O'Toole's proud grin still in his mind, he cantered his horse down the trail to Red Butte.

11

Slocum was enjoying his moment of peace and relative quiet in the back room of the Broken Dollar Saloon. His cigar was only half smoked, and he had plenty of liquor, though he didn't want or even need much of that. It was good to be alone. Often he found he could think better when he was like this, practicing card hands. His mind seemed in one way to be able to relax, and in another way it allowed fresh thinking to appear.

It all seemed to fit, the Kilrain part. He'd been back in town only a day since bringing in the wild horses, nearly all of them now at least partially broken in. And as his hands moved the cards about on the table, his thoughts ran through the whole Grady affair, as he was referring to it in his mind. The Kilrain bubble had blown right up. Every hour now, new revelations were coming out—how indeed he had headed the bandits, how Dutch Minetta and three others traveling with the McCone wagon train had, on Kilrain's orders, murdered and robbed the lot. Not a soul had escaped, and nearly all had been mutilated, mostly by Dutch, who not so incidentally had a record of cannibalism from many years back; though there had been no actual cannibalism with the McCone party. Dutch and his fellow murderers had all been killed at the fight in the canyon. There was an election for sheriff coming up.

It developed that Clyde Dancey had died of wounds he received at the box canyon fight. But Big Jaw Turk Nosniffer was supposed to be back in town, and the rumor was he intended to run for sheriff. No one had seen or heard anything of Sonny Clifford. He'd not shown up at the Double Box, nor had he appeared in town. A number of Kilrain's other gunmen had also vanished. The West was a big place.

Suddenly Slocum remembered the little locket. He put down his cards and reached into his shirt pocket and took it out.

He had tried a few times to open it, without any success. Now he finally did take his skinning knife to it and began to pry carefully. He realized the little locket was pure gold and obviously someone's special treasure, and he was afraid of damaging it if he wasn't careful. Even with the knife point he couldn't pry the lid open.

He was still trying to open it when there was a knock on the door. When he said, "Come," Boge Grady walked in.

Slocum slipped the locket into his pocket as he greeted the rancher.

"Well, Slocum, it looks like I'm out of the woods, thanks to you. Here's your pay and a bonus along with it." He put down a package in front of the deck of cards.

"Appreciate that, Boge."

"Can I buy you one?"

"Why not?" Slocum grinned.

There was another knock on the door. It was Felix O'Toole.

"Well," said Boge Grady, "looks like things are clearing. I do not believe Turk Nosniffer has a chance in hell of getting elected sheriff. Hell, as a deputy of Lupis Kilrain, his reputation stinks to hell and back."

"Who else you got?" Slocum asked. He grinned suddenly. "Might I suggest this young man right here?" Reaching over, he laid his big hand on Felix O'Toole's shoulder.

"Not on your life!" cried O'Toole in alarm. "I may be dumb in the ways of the West, but I am not crazy!"

His two companions were still roaring with laughter when the bartender brought in another bottle, courtesy of Boge Grady.

"You've got good social manners," Felix O'Toole said suddenly to the rancher.

Grady took the cigar out of his mouth. "That's nice to know," he said. He looked at Slocum then. "You said you'd had a recount on the stock. My tally has been two hundred forty-eight all along. I checked with Duncan. He came up with the same. It's one helluva big horse herd."

"I know," Slocum said, laying the palms of his hands flat on the table and leaning forward slightly. "But I've been told this morning's count is two forty-nine. What do you think of that?"

"You mean one of them mares foaled?"

Slocum grinned. "One of them mares not only foaled, but I hear she foaled the cutest little buckskin pony anybody ever did lay eyes on."

Grady let out a hoot and suddenly slapped his hand on the table, almost upsetting the drinks. "You mean—"

"I mean, it sure looks like that big buck has been doing his duty. And you're a lucky man, Mr. Bogardus Grady." He squinted at the ceiling as though having just thought of something. Looking again directly at the rancher, he said, "Or maybe I should say Miss Sandy Grady is a very lucky young lady. Boge, you haven't got a chance in a million of keeping that colt!"

They were still laughing heartily when Boge Grady took his leave.

"Good drinking, Slocum," he said, "but I better get back to business."

"Good to get the kinks out, Boge, with some drinks and a few laughs. You take care of the colt. I know you will."

Grady's tone was rueful as he said with a smile, "And I reckon I know—we both know—the new owner, she will."

He walked to the door, and turned. "I'll see you 'fore you ride out, Slocum. But what about Clifford? I heard he took off right after the canyon fight. Left the country."

"I doubt that. But we'll see."

Grady seemed to hesitate. "I can send in some men," he said.

"Then he won't show up. Leave it. I'll handle it."

"You sure, John?"

"That is a helluva dumb question."

Boge Grady nodded. "Gotcha!"

When the door closed behind him Felix O'Toole said he also had to leave.

"Sweetheart?"

A sigh took over the little man's entire body.

"Keep making that good money," Slocum said.

Felix O'Toole's eyes disappeared completely behind his spectacles as he beamed. "Nothing can beat old-world craftsmanship," he said. He was whistling softly to himself as he went out.

Slocum realized that Boge Grady hadn't fully understood Sonny Clifford's role. His dislike of the man was too great for him to see clearly that Clifford had been the big factor in helping Kilrain; and likely not only with the horse hunt. There was no doubt in the rancher's mind that with the death of Kilrain and the wiping out of his gang he was free of whatever it was that Clifford was after; in other words, without Kilrain and his men, Clifford was toothless. Probably he had left the country.

Slocum thought otherwise, but he hadn't pressed the point to Grady. He had known from the very beginning that it would be himself who would deal with the Englishman. There didn't have to be any reason. He just knew it. It was just this sort of intuitive way of knowing that had helped him out of more than one scrape. And if it helped him out of this situation, that was fine. If it didn't, that was fine too.

He wasn't at all surprised when there came another knock at the door. He waited a couple of beats before answering. A few of Clifford's henchmen? He wouldn't come in person. But he was surprised when he saw who walked in.

"For Christ's sake," he said, "can't Clifford think up a new act?"

Sweetheart Moon was carrying a bottle of Champagne, and she looked hurt at the way Slocum greeted her.

"Mr. Clifford sent this with his compliments," she said. "And if you feel like company, I've been sent with his compliments too."

"Where is Felix?"

"Felix?"

"Yeah, Felix."

"Ah yes, the Golden Eagle." She smiled, putting the bottle on the table and standing close to him.

"He'd make you a good man," Slocum said. "Though I can't say it the other way around."

"Getting pretty stiff in your old age, sir," she said with a marvelously teasing smile. "I never would have taken you for the permanent type."

"Then don't start now. I was talking about O'Toole. As for you, you cute thing, I'm ready any time you are; but it will be not when you call the deal, but when I do. Now leave, Sweetheart."

He could see she didn't like it, but she didn't leave immediately. Straightening up somewhat from the slouch she'd gone into, she said, "Mr. Clifford wants to see you. He's at his office in the Chicago House."

Slocum said, "You can tell him it's just as far from him to me as it is from me to him. I'll be here for another hour."

As he said those words he was out of his chair with the Colt drawn covering the girl. "Not a sound out of you!"

"What the hell you doin'?"

"Shut up!"

He was near the wall alongside but not close to the door of the room.

"It's damn quiet, isn't it?"

"I don't know what you mean." Her face was burning and he could see she was badly frightened.

"Seems every time we meet you're pulling some trick—the same trick."

"I'm not pulling anything, Slocum! Will you let me go?"

"Be quiet."

"Please!"

But he waved his hand, trying to hear what was outside the door.

In a moment he heard Clifford's voice. "Slocum! I'd like to talk to you. Can I come in?"

He looked at the girl. "Thought you could set it up, huh? Meet him over at the Chicago House. We know how far I would have gotten!"

"I don't know what you mean! I was only doin' what he told me. He said if I didn't they'd beat me up."

"Who?"

"Some men he had."

Clifford was calling again. "Slocum, I am not armed. Can I come in?"

"Nosniffer, was it? Big Jaw?"

"Yeah, yeah, that one with the big jaw like a hammer." She sniffed. "He was around there. At the Chicago House."

"All right, Clifford. You can come in. Alone."

"I am alone. And I am not armed."

The knob turned and the door opened, and Sonny Clifford walked into the room.

"How do you do," he said, looking at Sweetheart Moon as though he'd never seen her before.

Sweetheart Moon said nothing. She was rooted to the floor, her face white.

"Shut the door," Slocum said, still holding the gun on Clifford.

When the Englishman had done so, he walked to the

table, glanced down at the cards, and said, "I would prefer to talk privately with you, Slocum. We've a great deal to discuss. In private. Uh—if this young lady would excuse us."

"So long, Sweetheart," Slocum said. "And tell whoever's out there not to disturb me and Clifford here."

The Englishman smiled. "There is no one out there, Slocum. At least there wasn't when I came in."

"Oh, I do think there is," Slocum said as the door closed behind Sweetheart Moon. He crossed the room to sit down facing Sonny Clifford, at the same time holstering his sixgun. "A feller like you never makes a move without being covered."

Clifford smiled thinly. He sat forward in his chair on the other side of the table from Slocum. "I've come to offer you a job, Slocum. I've got big plans."

"For the railroad spur?"

The Englishman smiled carefully. "You are quick, Slocum. And it's that I appreciate. Just that."

"Your plan—if it is the railroad spur—isn't going anywhere without Grady's range, his land."

"You can help me get it."

"Kilrain couldn't help you, and he had a whole army of gunmen."

"I'd like you to think it over." Clifford stood up slowly. "I can be reached at the Chicago House. Take your time, but not too long. A day, two days. We'll have another talk." He paused on his way to the door. "By the way, you've spent some time with Miss Sandra Grady. She was on the horse hunt. I feel sure you must think highly of her." With a little nod he opened the door and started out.

Slocum stood up, catching the crude threat. He

sensed what was coming, but he wasn't sure just how Clifford would play it.

Suddenly the Englishman stopped right in the doorway and turned back into the room. His eyes were on the cards lying on the table. He was smiling as he pointed at one of the four poker hands Slocum had dealt himself.

"It looks to me like that one's going to be the winning hand when you show." He reached out his hand. "Mind if I take a look, Mr. Slocum?" His voice lifted on those last two words.

In the split second that Clifford reached for the card he stepped swiftly out of line with the door. Slocum saw that his hands were empty, but in the next second or two the derringer was in his fist, and he had dropped to the floor with the table between himself and Slocum. At the very same instant Big Jaw Turk Nosniffer stepped into the room with his .45 throwing lead.

Only Slocum wasn't there. At the instant that he caught Clifford's play, he was already drawing as he dropped flat on the floor, shooting Big Jaw right in his belly; then rolling, slamming three heavy slugs right through the table and into Sonny Clifford while the Englishman's bullet sailed harmlessly into the ceiling.

Outside in the saloon Sweetheart Moon walked to the bar. She was shaking.

"Gimme a drink," she said to the bartender. "And for God's sake don't tell me what happened in there."

In a few moments, when she heard Slocum's voice coming up behind her, she fainted.

"How the hell did you know Clifford was going to make his play like that?" Boge Grady asked as they stood at the fence watching the young buckskin colt's wobbly run.

"I didn't. But I knew he might be attracted to the cards, especially since some of the hands I dealt out were kind of crazy. And I knew he was wearing a hold-out. I just didn't know he had a gun up there instead of an ace or a wild card."

"But how did you know he was wearing the hold-out?" the rancher persisted.

"See, Clifford was a dude. Always dressed neat, his clothes tight on him."

"And . . . ?"

"And this time he was wearing a loose coat." He grinned. "And hell, not only that; Big Jaw—why, I'll bet you could hear him breathing in the middle of a herd of buffalo."

"Admiring my young friend, gentlemen?" said a familiar voice behind them.

Slocum turned slowly, enjoying every second of the anticipation of seeing Sandy Grady again.

"We are admiring *your* young friend, Sandy," her father said with a smile, turning back to the buckskin colt.

"Is it all over?" the girl asked, and Slocum heard the catch in her voice.

"It's all over," he said. "Except for this," he added, reaching to his shirt pocket.

He handed the little gold locket to Boge Grady. "I finally got this opened without breaking it. Does it look at all familiar?"

As the rancher took it, Slocum watched the expression on his face, an expression almost of disbelief as he opened the locket and looked at the picture inside.

"My God, Slocum. My God. I can't believe it!"

"What is it?" asked the girl, and he handed her the open locket.

"It's—someone, someone..." He was not able to finish.

Slocum watched him fight down any more expression of his feeling than just that little stumbling. It was a lot.

"She is very beautiful," Slocum said.

Grady nodded, his eyes squinting into the lowering sun that was almost at the horizon. "She was just a young girl then. And she's just a young girl now." He turned to face Slocum. "They stole that, along with some other things, quite a while back. I was real mad. Fact, that's what started me out to get Kilrain and the rest of 'em."

"They dropped it—one of them—out at the McCone wagon train," Slocum said, anticipating one of the Gradys asking how it had come into his hands.

Grady was looking down at the open locket again. Slocum and the girl were watching him. He closed the locket and looked at them both.

"I'll say thanks for that, Slocum."

Slocum nodded.

"And, Sandy...someday I'll give you this, but I'd like to carry it just a while longer," Grady said.

They watched him as he walked back to the ranch house. At the door he called back, "Come on in for a drink and supper when you've a mind to."

"Be there directly," Slocum called back.

"You'll be leaving," Sandy said.

Later, long after they'd had supper, they lay together under the starry sky and brought each other to a sweet climax.

"I guess it's just as well you're leaving," she said, lying in his arms.

And after they had had each other again she said,

"You know what I really love about you, John Slocum?"

"No, I don't know. Maybe everything, huh?" he said, tickling her ear with the tip of his tongue.

"I love the way you take your time making love."

"Maybe I'll take my time about leaving," he said.

She was already gasping as he began playing with her. "Oh, I just love the way you make love."

Slocum kissed the lobe of her ear. "As a friend of mine says, 'You just can't beat old world craftsmanship.'"

JAKE LOGAN